Luke s... at her question

Theresa had just asked him if his apartment in New Orleans really did have a spare bedroom.

"Yes, it does," he said at last, his voice flat and noncommittal. "Why? Don't you have a place to stay?"

"Of course, I do," she said. "I have a hotel reservation I'll have to cancel."

"I see. So you'd rather stay with me. Why? Do you want my company, or are you only interested in playing watchdog?"

"Does it matter?" Theresa snapped.

"No, I guess not. But I don't want you hovering over me like a mother hen. If someone is really after me, I intend to run him ragged, not hole myself up. Is that clear?"

"Yes, Luke," Theresa said quickly, relieved that he had not questioned her motives further....

KATHERINE ARTHUR is full of life. She describes herself as a writer, research associate (she works with her husband, a research professor in experimental psychology), farmer, housewife, proud mother of five and a grandmother to boot. The family is definitely full of overachievers. But what she finds most interesting is the diversity of occupations the children have chosen—sports medicine, computers, finance and neuroscience (pioneering brain tissue transplants), to name a few. Why, the possibilities for story ideas are practically limitless.

Books by Katherine Arthur

HARLEQUIN ROMANCE
2755—CINDERELLA WIFE
2821—ROAD TO LOVE
2905—FORECAST OF LOVE
2948—SEND ME NO FLOWERS
2971—REMEMBER IN JAMAICA
2991—THROUGH EYES OF LOVE

LOVING DECEIVER

Katherine Arthur

Harlequin Books

TORONTO • NEW YORK • LONDON
AMSTERDAM • PARIS • SYDNEY • HAMBURG
STOCKHOLM • ATHENS • TOKYO • MILAN

Original hardcover edition published in 1989
by Mills & Boon Limited

ISBN 0-373-03014-2

Harlequin Romance first edition November 1989

The world's a stage, and life's a play,
One rule all else above:
A hero needs a heroine.
He needs a script for love.
Barbara Ericksen

CHAPTER ONE

THE TALL man hung his coat next to Theresa's in the minuscule closet of Room F on the southbound *City of New Orleans* as if his staying were a foregone conclusion.

'In case you're interested,' he said, turning to face her, 'there is no longer any Mrs Lucas Thorndike.' He raised one dark eyebrow questioningly, deep brown eyes studying Theresa's face intently. 'Or had you already heard?'

'No, but I'm not surprised. And I'm not even *slightly* interested,' Theresa Long replied, meeting his gaze for a moment and then looking quickly away, erratic sensations inside her chest giving the lie to her statement. She pointed at the door, her finger trembling slightly. 'Put your coat back on and get out of here, Luke. This is my compartment and I am not going to share it with you or anyone else. Especially you.'

'But, as you can plainly see, my ticket says I'm entitled to be here,' Lucas Thorndike replied calmly, ignoring the finger and thrusting the ticket in front of Theresa.

Theresa pushed his hand away. 'It's not my fault that some idiot made a mistake,' she snapped. A feeling of desperation made beads of perspiration form on her upper lip. Of all the people on earth, why did Luke Thorndike have to be the one who got a duplicate ticket to her compartment? After five long years she did not need him dropping back into her life, like a spider suddenly appearing in front of her on its filament to startle her out of her relatively tranquil existence.

Luke smiled, the crinkly lines about his eyes that Theresa had once thought so adorable coming into full play.

'I know what you're thinking,' he said. He switched his velvet voice to raspy. 'Of all the compartments in all the trains in all the train stations in the world, why did he have to show up in mine?'

The perceptiveness of Luke's parody sent a chill through Theresa's taut nerves. 'Lousy Bogart,' she said, although it had been a quite passable imitation. 'Lousier coincidence. Why don't you get off and try again tomorrow? Take a plane?'

Luke looked wounded. 'You know I don't fly. Surely you haven't forgotten everything about me. Besides...' he gestured towards the window, 'we're moving. Too late to get off.'

'I'll push,' Theresa offered, briefly allowing herself the grim satisfaction of imagining herself flinging the handsome man bodily from the train. It was not, unfortunately, a viable solution to her problem. She clenched her fists tightly at her sides. 'Look, Luke, I don't care what you told the steward, we are *not* going to work this out so that you share my bedroom. You may as well head for the lounge car right now. I do remember that you like to drink.'

'"Don't tarry long," said Terry Long,' Luke rhymed. He shook his head. 'I don't think I'd enjoy twelve hours in the lounge car. I've sworn off the hard stuff, ever since I got rid of the chief cause of my aggravation. Sonya and I parted company about two years ago.' He squeezed past Theresa and sat down, sighing heavily. 'Three years of trying to make a go of it and failing, over a year to get an equitable settlement, and the past few months spent deciding what I wanted to do with the rest of my life. That about brings things up to date.' His mouth twisted into a wry smile. 'Five years of my life, summarised in one sentence.'

'How sad,' Theresa said unsympathetically. 'I suppose two Academy Awards for best screenplay don't count.' She had deliberately avoided reading any Hollywood gossip, not wanting to know what Luke was doing or who he was doing it with, but it had been impossible to miss the headlines about Luke's triumphs.

'Two separate lives,' Luke replied, 'the successful one an escape from the other. I don't suppose you'd understand. Your life is doubtless all of a piece.'

'It's not an unfamiliar pattern,' Theresa said, annoyed that he thought her so naïve. Her brother, in fact, often accused her of overworking to compensate for her lack of a love-life, something he occasionally tried to remedy by introducing her to eligible men. She doubted, however, that work had been Luke's only escape from an unhappy marriage. 'I do find it difficult to believe,' she said pointedly, 'that writing was your only outlet.'

Luke's dark eyes flashed with anger. For a moment Theresa thought she had gone too far and braced herself for a biting comeback. But, after a brief pause, he said simply, 'Then try harder.' He looked out of the window, and when he looked back his expression had cleared. 'Enough of dredging up the morbid past,' he said. 'Today is what we have to work with. And tomorrow.'

Theresa felt an agonising tension in every muscle as he shook off his dark mood and smiled that slow, warm smile that had so easily devastated the heart of a twenty-one-year-old girl. He was still the most handsome man she had ever seen, the brooding darkness of his angular features transformed with an inner light when he smiled. He gestured to the seat opposite him.

'Sit down and tell me, pretty Terry Long with the long, golden hair, what it is that keeps your cheeks so pink and your eyes so blue? Is it that exciting, living in Chicago and working for your brother's detective agency? You see, I haven't forgotten about you. And, unlike you, I am absolutely delighted at this coincidence which has brought us together again.'

Theresa tightened her lips and eyed Luke warily. He was still as glib and charming as ever, but she was not going to let him slither back into her life like a velvet-voiced snake.

'This is not a coincidence,' she said, 'this is a visitation for some wrong I've committed. Why don't you leave so I can examine my life for the cause?'

Luke chuckled. 'Still as delightfully tart-tongued as ever. With that sweet face of yours, one tends to expect baby cereal instead of lemon juice. Do sit down, Terry love, and let us discuss our mutual problem. As I recall, there are two bunks that appear like magic in here at night.'

'I am not sitting,' Theresa snapped, 'and don't call me "love". Just get out of here. There is no way I am going to share this room with you.' The very thought of listening to Luke breathe and mumble in his sleep all night only a few feet away from her made her feel woozy, as if she were back in the cabin of that little sail-boat . . .

'I can't bear the thought of you standing there like that for twelve hours,' Luke said, puckering his forehead into an exaggerated frown. 'There you'll be in the morning, rigid as a statue, those lovely eyes frozen into an unseeing stare. I'll have to tuck you under my arm like a two-by-four and carry you off the train, being careful not to hit your head . . .'

'Oh, shut up!' Theresa shouted. Luke's favourite trick was to turn everything into a fantastic story, something that was marvellous when it involved his screen writing, but was going to drive her crazy if he did it to her now, the way he had in California during that magical month when she fell in love with him.

'Then sit down,' Luke said, just the faintest edge of authority in his velvety voice. 'Or I'll make you,' he added, leaning forward.

'Don't touch me,' Theresa warned. She edged to her seat and perched on it, every muscle tense. 'What in the world were you doing in Chicago, anyway? And why are you going to New Orleans?'

'That's better,' Luke said, leaning back and smiling. 'The little detective goes to work. Well, Miss Holmes, I was in Chicago getting some materials together for a story I'm going to write while I'm in New Orleans. A friend offered me the loan of his apartment in the French Quarter, and I thought it the perfect oppor-

tunity to get away to a place where I knew not a soul
and get some work done. I thought of looking you
up yesterday, but I was afraid I might not get a very
warm reception. Alas, I guess I was right. But now
that we are together, can't we just let bygones be bygones? As I recall, we did have rather a good thing
going until you found out that I was married, and
therefore an evil monster like your ne'er-do-well
father.'

'No, we can't,' Theresa said flatly, trying not to
show the agony that Luke's reminder brought back
so vividly. She had never told him of her love for him,
although he doubtless had guessed she was more involved than he'd wanted when she'd flung her angry
accusations at him the day she'd found out that he
was married. 'I don't want anything to do with a man
whose principles, or lack of them, allowed him to
behave as if he weren't married. I've seen too much
of what that kind of thing does to people since I've
been working for Quentin. It may be pretty common,
but that doesn't mean I have to accept it.'

Luke pulled on his ear and looked sideways at
Theresa. 'I see that time has done nothing to soften
your attitude. I might point out that Sonya had
already started wandering, and that all I ever asked
of you was companionship. I still don't feel that I was
entirely in the wrong.' He turned the full intensity of
his dark, deep-set eyes on Theresa. 'Being with you
that month did a lot to save my sanity. I don't take
rejection well, and Sonya's behaviour had me feeling
pretty low. Knowing that you could like me for the
man I was without any of the Hollywood tinsel and
glitter gave me the courage to go back and try to solve

what turned out to be an insoluble problem. Of course, it was a bit of a setback when you got so angry, but at least I understood why you did.'

Did he really? Theresa wondered. Did he have any idea how deeply she had been hurt?

'That still doesn't make what you did all right,' she said, trying to keep the bitterness from her voice. She did not want him to know how much his presence still disturbed her. In addition to the anger, there was still a strong, undeniable attraction that was sending such contradictory signals to her brain that she felt hot and cold at the same time. 'You shouldn't have needed a twenty-one-year-old to tell you to try harder to make your marriage work, instead of seeking solace elsewhere,' she said, trying to sound firm and positive.

'Theresa,' Luke said seriously, 'I did not need you to tell me that. Otherwise, a lot more would have happened between us than did, and I might have been the philanderer that you think I was.'

Theresa eyed him suspiciously. Why was he trying so hard to convince her now that he had been a paragon of a husband in recent years? He hadn't bothered to deny her accusations before. 'I'm happy to hear that you reformed,' she said tightly. 'Not many wandering husbands do.'

For a moment Luke looked as if he were going to issue another denial. Then suddenly he chuckled softly. 'Tell me, Theresa,' he said, 'why didn't you marry poor Carl Weidenkamp? He was madly in love with you, and he'd never have wandered farther than the nearest health club.'

'How did you know about him?' Theresa demanded, startled that Luke had apparently been keeping far better track of her than she had imagined. Her brother had introduced her to Carl, a young stockbroker whose talk of million-dollar deals had temporarily dazzled her. When she'd discovered that his values were so typically yuppie—those of a young, upwardly mobile professional—that she could always tell what his answer to a question would be before she asked it, she quickly lost interest in him and broke off their relationship.

'Elementary, my dear. Elementary,' Luke replied, looking mysterious. 'Carl's boss used to be my broker and good friend, before he came to take over the Chicago branch of the firm. When he told me one of his rising young stars was dating an adorable detective, with serious intent, I put two and two together. I met Carl a few months ago when I was in town. Struck me as a dreadful bore.'

Theresa frowned. Something did not ring true. If Carl had met the famous Lucas Thorndike, he would have told her about it in glowing detail.

'You never met Carl,' she said accusingly, 'or he would have said so. He's very impressed by celebrities.'

Luke's grin was positively evil. 'Did he mention meeting a talent scout named Marcus Flint?'

'Oh, God,' Theresa said, biting her lip to keep from laughing. Carl had rambled on and on about how impressed one Marcus Flint had been with his physique, how he might want to use him in a commercial for men's underwear. The mirth bubbling in Luke's eyes was too much for her and she burst out laughing. 'That was a terrible trick to pull on poor Carl,' she scolded, at the same time thinking hypocritically that it was such a perfect one it was incredible.

'But he deserved it,' Luke said, nodding knowingly. 'There. Now that I've got you in a reasonably good humour, let's get down to business here. There's no reason we can't share this room, is there? We can talk about old times, have a glass of wine together, and at bedtime you can have whichever bunk you like. I promise to be a perfect gentleman at all times. Agreed?'

'No!' Theresa said, feeling her tension return. She was not going to sit here and let Luke's easy charm turn her insides into jelly, as they had before. Once he got her laughing with him, it could be all too easy. She loved to laugh, and had never since laughed as much as she had with Luke. More recently, laughter had been at something of a premium. Carl had been rather humourless, probably one of the reasons she had felt safe with him, she realised now. He was so completely unlike Luke that he had never had any chance of destroying her defences with wit and humour.

Luke frowned. 'Theresa, you're not being reasonable. As I recall, you prided yourself on having much more of that quality than I do. Not to mention intelligence, honesty, common sense and morals.'

Theresa winced inwardly. Luke certainly remembered some of the items she had dwelt on at length when she'd so angrily lashed out at him for deceiving her. And, from his point of view, he was perfectly right about being reasonable. He could spend the evening chatting casually, and then go his merry way in the morning, no worse for wear. She, on the other hand, might have quite a hangover from the experience, even without any wine.

'I am being perfectly reasonable,' she replied, hoping she sounded more calm and reasonable than she felt. 'I took the train because I wanted to be alone for a while. I've been working hard, and I have a hard job ahead of me in New Orleans. I don't feel like talking.'

'So? I'll be quiet,' Luke said with a shrug. He cocked his head and frowned. 'I am curious, though, about what takes you to New Orleans.'

'A search for a wandering husband,' Theresa replied, with a meaningful lift of her eyebrows. 'The world seems to be full of them. And wandering wives too, I'm afraid.'

'I see.' Luke sighed. 'Moral decay is all around us. It makes good story material, but it's bad news on the home front, isn't it? I suppose seeing so much of it, combined with your father's disappearing act, makes a sweet innocent like yourself even less willing to have anything to do with someone she still mistakenly considers a reprobate. Especially since you seem to be carrying a bit of a torch. I could be dangerous.'

'I am *not* carrying a torch!' Theresa denied hotly. 'The fact that I haven't forgotten what you did does not add up to carrying a torch at all!'

'Then why are you so afraid to let me stay here tonight? You know perfectly well that if I say I'll be a gentleman, I will, whether you want me to or not. You've tested that out very thoroughly before.' Luke raised his black eyebrows and fixed Theresa with a penetrating stare.

'I am not afraid . . .' Theresa began, knowing full well that she was terrified, and cursing the fact that she could not force her eyes to meet Luke's un-flinching gaze. Before she could finish, there was a knock on the door.

'That will be the steward,' Luke said softly. 'Well? What's the verdict?'

'Oh, all right, you can stay,' Theresa growled, not looking at him. She grabbed her bag and flung the strap over her shoulder. 'I'm going to the lounge car for a while. You stay here,' she ordered before opening the door. To the steward's questioning look she said abruptly, 'He's staying. Which way is the lounge car?'

'Four cars ahead,' the steward replied, looking curiously at Theresa's flushed face.

'Thanks,' she said, and pushed past him into the hallway.

When she reached the lounge car, she bought a large Coke at the snack bar and then went on into the seating area. There was only one completely vacant table, and she sat there, next to the window, with her back towards a middle-aged couple sitting at the far side of the table behind her. Apparently, she thought grimly, this was as close as she was going to get to being alone on this trip. What a bizarre coincidence that Luke Thorndike should show up at her door. His paraphrase of the Bogart line had certainly been apt. But then, lack of perceptiveness had not been one of Luke's faults. If anything, he was too perceptive, worming his way into your very soul by pulling you along with him into a world of his own invention, where all the rules were his, too. It was so much easier to confess to all of your hopes and fears when you were on another planet. That was where he had taken her that first night in California...

She had been visiting her mother, who had moved to Pasadena to be near her sister after Theresa's father had left his family in Chicago for an unknown destination with one of a seemingly endless series of attractive younger women. Theresa's brother, Quentin, had at first searched unsuccessfully for their father in his spare time, then decided to become a full-time private investigator. His business had thrived, and Theresa had decided to join him. She had specialised in criminology at college and, after a post-graduation visit to her mother, would be ready to return to Chicago and join Quentin's A-1 Detective Agency as a fully fledged private investigator.

A college friend from California, Lisa Mattingly, had told Theresa to call her when she got there, and she'd show her around. Theresa had known that Lisa came from a wealthy family, but she was overwhelmed by the luxury of the Mattinglys' Beverly Hills home, and the star-studded post-production party to which she was invited. Lisa's father, Joel Mattingly, was the producer, and Lucas Thorndike the writer, of a movie that both men expected to receive an Academy Award nomination.

Theresa had spotted Luke Thorndike across the Mattinglys' patio, entranced by the dark, brooding handsomeness of the tall, slender man with jet-black hair. She thought he must be a star, but could not remember seeing him before. When he caught her looking at him and smiled slowly, she felt her knees go weak.

'Who is that man?' she asked Lisa. 'Is he a new star that I haven't seen yet?'

'No, he's a screenwriter. Lucas Thorndike. Dad says he's a genius,' Lisa said in awed tones, before introducing Theresa to Luke. 'A little crazy, but a genius. He's only twenty-nine, but Dad says he's a dead cert for the award for the best original screenplay this year.'

After they were introduced, Luke stared at Theresa for so long without saying anything that she began to think his mind had slipped a cog.

'I heard you were a genius,' she said finally, to break the tension that was building between them. 'Say something brilliant.'

'E equals mc squared?' he volunteered hopefully, his eyebrows raised so comically that Theresa burst into helpless giggles.

'You're not a physicist, silly,' she said. 'You're a writer.'

'Oh, yes, I forgot for a moment,' he replied. Then he shook his head. 'But I must be a physicist. How else could I have gotten on to this ridiculous planet?' He looked over his shoulder. 'I wonder where I parked my spaceship. I hope none of these Earthlings has taken it. I don't trust them.' He looked back at Theresa. 'Do you?' he asked. 'Or are you one of them?'

'I'm not sure,' Theresa replied, immediately caught up in Luke's fantasy world. 'Sometimes I think I am, and sometimes not. How can I tell for sure?'

'Very difficult,' Luke replied, now looking intensely serious. 'Very difficult, indeed. There is one test, though, that I could give you that would tell. Would you like to take it?'

'Is it dangerous?' Theresa asked breathlessly, entranced by the dark, sparkling depths of Luke's eyes.

'Not a bit. You only need answer one question.' He bent closer. 'Of course, the answer to that one question may change your entire life. Are you game?'

'By all means,' Theresa replied, unaware of the prophetic nature of Luke's statement. 'This may be my only chance to find out the truth.'

'Very well. The question is this.' He looked over his shoulder again and then took Theresa's arm, leading her away from the crowd to a spot beneath a palm tree. 'Wouldn't want them to hear and find out the secret,' he said in low tones. 'The question,' he repeated, 'is ... would you rather spend the evening with this overdressed, overpaid crowd of phonies, or would you rather put on your jeans and go with me to a place where they serve fish and chips and ice-cold beer in frosted mugs? Choose carefully, now. The answer forever seals your fate.'

Theresa was dimly aware that she was being treated to a very sophisticated come-on, but she was so entranced that she did not hesitate.

'The second alternative sounds much better,' she replied. 'I'd choose it.'

'Thank goodness,' Luke said, sighing as if greatly relieved. 'You're not one of them.' He smiled conspiratorially. 'One of the best things about not being one of them is that we can say goodbye and leave, and not one of them will guess what we're up to. They'll think I've decided to seduce you, or do some of those other disgusting things that Earthling men and women do when they're alone together. They'll never guess we're just going to talk and get acquainted and have a good time doing it.'

'And is that what we're going to do?' Theresa asked, feeling a little shiver of excitement rush through her.

'Precisely,' Luke answered, taking her arm again. 'Observe my perfect Earthling manners when we take our leave.'

They *were* perfect, as Luke had said, and, as he had predicted, Theresa could see that the 'Earthlings' at the party looked at her knowingly, suspecting that her virtue, if she had any, was about to be violated by the handsome writer. She was rather apprehensive herself, as they got into what Luke called his private starship, a silver Porsche.

'I'm afraid I don't have any jeans with me,' she said, as he gunned the car away from the Mattinglys' mansion.

'Neither do I,' Luke replied with an easy grin, 'but if we say we're wearing jeans, then we are. We can pretend about things like that, but...' he gave Theresa a quick, serious look, 'unlike Earthlings, when we talk about ourselves and what we think, we don't pretend. We always tell the truth.'

That was one of the statements that Theresa threw back in Luke's face on that terrible night a month later when she found out that he was married. By then, she was completely under Luke's spell, so deeply in love with him that she thought of nothing else night and day. He had taken her all over southern California, to out of the way little bistros, secluded canyons, isolated beaches, windswept desert dunes. It had never occurred to her that he was keeping her out of sight, only that he preferred going to such places, where they could be alone. They talked endlessly, held hands and touched casually, but never made love.

Occasionally, Luke would say goodnight with a kiss that left Theresa soaring, as if she really were on another planet, but he always left immediately afterwards. When she asked him why, he told her that it was because he did not want her to think that he was turning into an Earthling, something that could happen if one were not very careful.

'I can feel myself wanting to do some of those terrible Earthling things,' he said, 'and the time is not right. Only when the time is right can we do them, and not be caught in their web.'

'When will the time be right?' Theresa asked, understanding only part of his meaning.

'Maybe soon. Maybe never,' Luke had replied, his expression guarded. 'It depends on many things.'

Now, as Theresa stared out the window of the train into the darkness of the autumn night, tears filled her eyes. If only she had understood all of what Luke had meant then, she might have saved herself the heartbreak she felt later. He had been trying to tell her that he didn't want to get too deeply involved with her. Maybe, in his strange way, he was telling her that he was already married. At the time, however, she had taken it only as a promise of things to come.

The morning of their last day together, Luke had been in high spirits. He had borrowed a small sailboat from a friend, for a trip to Catalina Island. 'To investigate the natives,' he said. 'And see where the buffalo roam.' He had spent the trip over concocting a wildly delightful story about how a Sioux Indian brave named Walks Far And Swims A Little had driven his herd of buffalo across the plains and mountains until he came to the Pacific Ocean. There, feeling it was time to swim a little, he had urged his herd into the sea, swimming after them until they reached Catalina Island. 'Which, if he'd thought about it,' Luke said, 'was really meant for cattle, not buffalo.'

'You mean I had to go through all of that for that terrible pun?' Theresa had cried, scooping a handful of water to throw at him, and laughing helplessly at the same time.

'I didn't think it was so bad,' Luke had said, looking hurt. 'Give me a chance. I can come up with a lot worse.'

And he had made a valiant attempt to do so all day, as they toured the interior of the small resort island, discovering, to Theresa's amazement, that there really were buffalo to be seen.

A storm had prevented their sailing back to the mainland, but there was a snug little cabin on the sailboat, and Luke had insisted they stay there. It was the first time they had spent a night together, and Theresa had been both anxious and excited, wondering if this might be the time that Luke would go further than a kiss. In her fantasies, he already had, many times, but she was not sure she wanted him to in reality, in spite of the deep longing that was her constant companion when they were together. To her distress, at first he did not even kiss her goodnight, even though she made it very obvious that she wanted him to. She stood close beside him in the little cabin, her face upturned to his, her eyes on the wide, gentle curves of his mouth. Instead of kissing her lips, he took her face between his hands and kissed the tip of her nose, then put his arms around her and held her close.

'Oh, Theresa,' he murmured in her ear, 'I'm so afraid of the way you make me feel. Don't tempt me too much. I don't want to do something we'll both regret.'

Theresa had got into her bunk, feeling confused and depressed. Why would making love to her be a cause for regret? Neither of them had any social disease, and she knew enough to protect herself from an unwanted pregnancy. She might still be a virgin, but she had made no vow to stay that way indefinitely; she simply hadn't been tempted to forsake that virtue for someone in whom she knew she had only a passing interest. With Luke, it was much more than that. She would gladly spend her life following him into those exotic flights of fancy that more often than not ended in deep, intelligent discussions of the real world, viewed from angles that Theresa had never seen before. As she lay in her bunk, her eyes filled with tears. Was there, she wondered, something about her that Luke did not like, after all? The tears aggravated her sinuses, and she fumbled for a Kleenex and blew her nose. Luke was by her side in a flash.

'What's wrong, love?' he asked, laying a cool hand on her cheek in the darkness. 'Don't tell me nothing is. I heard you tossing and turning over here.'

'I was just wondering,' she answered, honestly as he had prescribed, 'if there's something about me that you don't like.'

'Good lord, no,' he answered vehemently. 'I like everything about you, from your silky golden topknot to your little pink toes, and I like everything that's inside, too. I've never enjoyed anyone's company as much. You understand what I'm saying better than anyone, and you even laugh at my puns. What on earth makes you ask such a question? The fact that I haven't tried to seduce you?'

'I suppose that's it,' Theresa answered reluctantly. Putting it that way did sound rather cheap.

'Believe me,' Luke said, his voice a low growl, 'it isn't because I haven't wanted to.'

'Then what is it?'

For a long time Luke did not answer. Theresa could see his eyes searching her face and feel his warm breath upon her lips as he bent closer. Impulsively, she put her hand behind his head and buried it in his dark, thick hair, something she always longed to do but had seldom done before. It felt wonderful, silky and crisp and vibrant as Luke himself. Without even thinking, she pulled his head nearer until his lips touched hers.

'Theresa, don't,' he whispered, resisting momentarily. Then, with a groan, he lowered his head and let his arms find their way around her. He stretched out beside her on the narrow bunk, their bodies touching from head to toe.

Feeling Luke's kiss grow from a soft and tentative warmth to passionate heat sent Theresa's heart to pounding. The sensation of his hard, slender body against hers fired waves of longing that engulfed her. It seemed she could never be close enough to him, never belong to him as completely as she wanted. Her breasts felt swollen with wanting to have him possess them, and when his hand slowly pushed inside her shirt she made sounds of encouragement deep in her throat. He cupped her breast almost roughly.

'Is this what you want me to do?' he asked hoarsely, lowering his head to let his mouth find the rosy peaks his fingers had discovered.

'Oh, yes,' Theresa breathed, arching toward him eagerly, swept far beyond any planet in the sky by the yearning hunger with which Luke did her bidding. After he unzipped her jeans and pulled them off, she wriggled against the sheets in blissful anticipation while he removed his own clothing. Her arms welcomed his naked body back to meet her own and she pulled his hips against her, revelling in the knowledge of his hard arousal, wanting only to join with him and make their mutual longing culminate in the burst of ecstasy she was sure would come. For a few minutes, Luke moved against her, his mouth possessing hers with a wild eagerness, his hands clutching her to him as if he, too, was looking for a way to meld their bodies into one.

Then, suddenly, he rolled away from her and on to the floor of the cabin, swearing volubly in a language he later told Theresa was Greek.

'I will not do this! I will not!' he rasped in anguish when she asked, bewildered, what was wrong. 'This is not the time and not the place. You're not ready for this, and, God knows, I'm not either.' Nothing that Theresa could say produced any further explanation. All she could get was a growled, 'Go to sleep.'

The next morning, they were both in a terrible humour from lack of sleep. Luke tried to make some jokes about the wages of Earthling sins, but they fell flat. They went up on deck to prepare to leave, the bright sunshine seeming like a reproach for their dark-circled eyes. A man was strolling down the dock towards them, walking a small dog on a leash. He saw Luke and quickened his steps. Luke saw the man and turned his back, but it was too late.

'Hey, there, Luke Thorndike,' said the man. 'Avast, you old landlubber. What brings you and the missus to sunny Catalina? Oh, that's not Sonya, is it? Who's the pretty lady, you old sea-dog?'

'The missus? Sonya?' Theresa repeated, feeling the world reel around her. Luke had gone ghostly pale beneath his tan, leaving his skin looking grey and lifeless. His eyes, as he stared back at Theresa, looked like dark, desolate, bottomless pools.

Theresa still hated to remember that day. Luke, to his credit, had not said that he could explain everything. The only trite part of what he did say was that his wife didn't understand him, which was not terribly difficult to believe. He had listened patiently to Theresa's tearful ravings and accusations, his only argument being that she was too young to understand, just as he and his wife had been too young when they married.

'Twenty-one is foolishness with a licence,' he said.

'And what's so wonderful about twenty-nine?' she had countered.

'At the moment, I can't think of a thing,' he replied. 'It just lets you foresee the things that will go wrong before they do, thereby limiting the fun you have on the way.'

He gave Theresa time to get herself in control, and then took her to her mother's house.

'If you ever need me, just call. I'll be there in a flash,' he told her before she got out of his car.

'I won't,' she said. 'I don't ever want to see you again. I don't ever want to talk to you again.'

Luke had smiled at that. 'You'll see me again,' he promised. 'When the time is right, you'll see me again.'

For a long time Theresa had wondered what he meant by that, clinging to a vain hope that it meant he cared for her. But, as the years went by and she did not see him, she assumed it had just been something fanciful that he said because it sounded interesting and profound. Something he probably said to the next young woman he found to divert him until she discovered the truth. She had not heard of his divorce. She had avoided reading any Hollywood gossip. She did not want to be reminded of Luke Thorndike and that disastrous month when her heart had ruled her life. Was she still carrying a torch, as he had said? Had she still had some faint hope that he would keep his promise to see her again? Was that why she had let him stay, when common sense said it was the last thing she should do?

Theresa shook her head and stared glumly into her glass of Coke. Luke's statement had implied something planned, not a chance meeting due to someone's mistake. Apparently, for him, the time had never been right, and she would be a fool to think that serendipity would make it right. Even more a fool to want anything to do with him. He had already proved that he couldn't be trusted. Even if he had, in fact, deceived no one else, he had deceived her. There could be no right time for her to see him again. She had been successfully going about her own business for some time, and Luke was obviously going about his, with no thoughts of seeing Theresa Long in his plans. Seeing him again was only reopening old wounds. Her wounds, not his. The only sensible thing for her to do, now that she had stupidly agreed to let him share her compartment, was to stay in the lounge car until it was time for sleep, then climb into her bunk, go to sleep, and reverse the procedure as quickly as possible in the morning. Drat! What should have been a quiet, enjoyable trip had turned into a nightmarish disaster.

She poked disconsolately at the ice in her glass with the straw and looked around her. The other occupants of the lounge did not look especially interesting. Most of them looked as if they, too, were only passing the time until they got to New Orleans. Down by the bar, a tall man moved out of the way, and she caught sight of two short, rotund men she had seen earlier on the platform on her way to the train. They had been wearing identical black overcoats and hats. Hurrying along ahead of her, they had reminded her of two fat penguins in a rush for the sea.

The suits that the men wore were not identical as their overcoats had been, but they were, Theresa thought, equally distinctive. One was wearing a garish plaid, while the other wore a dark brown suit with a chalk-stripe. As they turned to enter the seating area, each clutching a drink, she could see that they were twins, their faces round, puffy, and rather threatening-looking, with squinty eyes and tight mouths. Tweedle-Dee and Tweedle-Dum play gangster, Theresa thought, wondering if that fancy came to her because of Luke's influence, or if she would have thought of it anyway. She looked studiously back at her glass, hoping that the pair would not decide to sit at her table. She might be tempted to ask which one was Tweedle-Dee and which Tweedle-Dum, something she doubted they would find amusing.

To her relief, the men went on by, instead taking the two chairs directly behind her. Apparently the couple who had been sitting there did not find their company compatible, for she heard them get up and leave moments later. Even though the men talked in low voices, they were so close behind her that she easily overheard everything they said. First they discussed a funeral they had recently attended, where the deceased had apparently suffered a violent death. Intrigued, Theresa listened more closely. The men had an assignment to carry out in New Orleans.

'It could mean a lot of running around,' one said. 'I hope my back don't act up.'

'We could just take him out on the train,' the other said. 'We saw him get on.'

'Nah, it's too messy,' the first one replied. 'Besides, the boss don't know he's here, and we're getting paid by the day. Why not get a vacation for free.'

Theresa felt a chill go through her and her ears perked up to their most acute. Had her impression of the men been that accurate? 'Take someone out' was gangland talk for killing someone. Were the two men hired assassins?

'Yeah, I guess you're right. I like New Orleans. Always plenty of action, and the weather's sure better. It's not like there's any danger of losing him. He don't know we're coming. He'll leave a trail like tyre tracks in the snow.'

The other man chuckled. 'From what I hear, Luke Thorndike wouldn't know what to do if he did know. He's one of them arty types with no common sense, if you know what I mean.'

Theresa felt her stomach go into a knot. Luke? Those awful men were after Luke? She fought down a sudden wave of light-headedness. This was no time to panic. She must find out more. Luke's life might depend on it. It was with mixed feelings that she heard one of the men behind her say, 'Hey, how about seeing if that cute little cookie behind us wants to chat a while? I can talk to you any old time.' The other man agreed, and before Theresa could brace herself any further, the men had got up and were standing by her table.

'Mind if we join you?' said the plaid-suited one. 'Seems a shame for such a pretty girl to be so lonesome.'

'Not at all,' Theresa said, managing to look pleased at the flattery. 'Are you going to New Orleans?'

'Yes, ma'am,' replied striped-suit. 'The Chicago weather's plum got us down. Need a bit of a change.'

'I know what you mean,' Theresa said, nodding. 'I nearly blew away, getting to the station this afternoon.'

They talked about the weather, about the men's twin status, and eventually Theresa led the conversation around to a discussion of New Orleans, under the guise that she might want to live there if she could find secretarial work.

'I've never seen anything but the French Quarter, and I know that would be too expensive for me,' she said. 'Are you two familiar with the city?'

'I am,' said a voice, and Theresa looked up to see Luke standing beside the table, holding a glass of wine. He sat down beside her. 'I didn't realise you didn't have a place to stay,' he said. To the two men, whose expressions had not changed an iota with Luke's arrival, he said, 'I met Miss Long earlier.' He returned his attention to Theresa. 'I have an apartment on Dumaine, with a spare bedroom. You'd be welcome to stay with me.'

The men chuckled simultaneously as Theresa frowned at Luke, although she was not frowning for the reason they thought. Good lord, Luke, she was thinking desperately, why not give them a key?

'I'd be glad to show you around,' Luke went on. 'Have you been to Preservation Hall? You mustn't miss the jazz there. It's the greatest, isn't it?' He looked at the twins for confirmation.

'You've got that right,' plaid suit agreed. 'I remember the first time I heard...'

The three men were soon involved in a lengthy discussion of jazz greats, followed by talk of some of the wonderful French and Cajun cuisine for which New Orleans is famous. Theresa felt as if she would fly apart, her nerves were so tense. Fate might have provided her with the chance to save Luke's life, but he was not doing anything to make the job easier. Luke, his usual friendly self, might as well be giving the two men an itinerary of his favourite spots, and there was no way to stop him without making the men suspicious. It was amazing to her that the twins were equally friendly, given their mission. No one, Luke especially, would ever guess that he was their target.

They must be real professionals, so used to their ugly work that it did not even faze them.

At last Luke finished his glass of wine.

'Well, I guess I'll turn in,' he said, rising. He nodded formally to Theresa. 'Goodnight, Miss Long.'

Still the perfect gentleman, Theresa thought grimly. He didn't want the twins to think she was in the same bedroom with him. But when the round little men got up to leave at the same time, she jumped from her chair as if propelled by jets.

'I think I'll retire, too,' she said, following closely behind the three men. There was no way on earth that she was going to let Luke out of her sight, no matter what anyone might think.

They stopped at the car before the one where Luke and Theresa were staying, saying goodnight as pleasantly, she thought, as if they were two preachers on vacation from their flocks.

The bunks were already made up in Room F. The moment they were inside and the door locked behind them, Theresa grabbed Luke's arm and pulled him over to sit on the lower bunk.

'Have you ever seen those twins before?' she asked.

Luke frowned. 'No, never. Quite a pair, aren't they? Why do you ask? Is something wrong?' He grinned. 'Did they jointly proposition you?'

'You would think of that,' Theresa snapped, her heart pounding in anxiety over what she had to say. 'Unfortunately, it's even worse than that. I've got something to tell you that you had better listen to very carefully.'

Luke cocked his head and looked at Theresa curiously. 'What's the matter, Terry, love?' he asked, taking hold of her clammy hands. 'You look pale. Are you that afraid of being alone with me? If you are, I'll leave.'

'Good heavens, no! That's the last thing I want!' At Luke's startled look, Theresa lowered her voice to a whisper. 'It's about those two men you were talking to. They're hired killers, and it's you they've been hired to kill.'

'Me?' Luke frowned, then his lips twitched. He burst out laughing. 'That's ridiculous! I may have written some plays that weren't great, but nothing that I should have to die for. Of course...' he chuckled again, 'there are some critics who might feel that I should.'

'Oh, Luke,' Theresa shook her head, pleading with her eyes for him to stop making jokes, 'this is serious. I'm not stupid and I'm not joking. When those men first came into the lounge car I thought they looked rather sinister, but I thought it was just my imagination working overtime. Sort of an occupational hazard of detectives. Then they sat down behind me, and I overheard everything they said. One of them suggested they "take you out on the train", but the other wanted to get paid for a few days in New Orleans, so they decided to wait. They said your name right out. Luke Thorndike. Unless there are two of you, they meant you.'

Luke's smile faded. 'You are serious, aren't you?'

Theresa nodded. 'Think. Is there anyone who hates you enough to want you dead? Is your ex-wife that angry with you?'

'Oh, hell, no,' Luke replied. 'She's already planning to get married again. I suppose it could be . . . no, that doesn't make sense.'

'Who? What doesn't make sense?' Theresa asked, leaning toward him.

'Big Joey Scarcelli. I owe him some money, but I told him I'd pay as soon as I finish this story I'm working on. If he got rid of me, he'd never collect.'

'Big Joey?' Theresa's voice cracked. 'You mean the Las Vegas kingpin? How did you ever get in debt to him?'

Luke shrugged. 'I got a little carried away one night, trying to double my money. He offered to lend me enough to keep going for a while.' He smiled wryly. 'It wasn't my night.'

'I didn't know you gambled,' Theresa said, frowning. 'I thought you didn't believe in it.'

'I didn't. I still don't. That's the only time I've ever been to Las Vegas. I had to go there to do some research, and I didn't think I could write about gambling without trying it.' He shook his head. 'I still can't believe that's the reason that strange-looking pair is after me. I can't believe they're killers. They look more like Tweedle-Dee and Tweedle-Dum.'

Theresa almost choked. 'That's exactly what I thought when I saw them,' she said. 'But I can't help what I heard. And I hate to tell you, but for Big Joey, the money isn't always the important thing. He sometimes has people—er—eliminated, just to set an example to others who don't pay their debts. Someone as well known as you are sets a terrific example.'

'Phew.' Luke looked down and stroked Theresa's hands, then looked up at her and smiled. 'I guess maybe I am in big trouble. What do I do? Learn to dodge bullets?'

'Very funny,' she said, shivering at the tingling sensations that were creeping up her arms from the warmth of Luke's hands on hers. 'I think it might be more practical to notify the authorities in New Orleans. Those men may be wanted for other crimes, and they can be picked up by the police before they have a chance to do anything.'

Luke looked thoughtful for a moment and then shook his head. 'I'm not sure how practical that is. As distinctive as that pair are, if there's any open charge against them, they'd never be able to leave their home. They're probably the kind you always see on television. You know, "here's Mick the Finger, reputed assassin for the mob". Always "reputed". When they get caught, it's for something dastardly, like driving without a licence. No, I think the only thing for me to do is to lock my door and try to sit with my back to a wall when I go out.' He grinned suddenly. 'It might be exciting, living the life of a marked man. I'll bet there's some good story material there.'

'Good story material? Dead men don't write stories,' Theresa exclaimed.

'And that would make a great title! Thank you, Theresa.' He pulled a notepad from his pocket. 'I'd better write that down.'

'Luke!' Theresa shook her head, watching him scribble on his notepad with a sinking heart. Luke was not taking her warning seriously. He would have been more frightened if she'd jumped out from behind a door and shouted, 'Boo!' Perhaps if she tried a more fanciful approach he would listen. When Luke had put the notepad back into his pocket she frowned at him.

'I don't believe you realise the gravity of your situation,' she said. 'Gangsters don't care a fig whether you're an Earthling or not. They have their own planet and their own rules, and if you don't play their game the way they want, they send you to the sidelines . . . permanently.'

Instead of looking worried, Luke smiled delightedly. 'You do remember. I was afraid maybe you were one of them, after all. They forget very quickly, you know. I was thinking that perhaps if I befriended Tweedle-Dee and Tweedle-Dum, they'd forget what they were sent to do. They actually seemed like pretty nice fellows.'

'Oh, Luke,' Theresa groaned, 'you can't be that stupid. Even Adolf Hitler could be a nice guy when it suited his purposes. Isn't there anything I can do to make you see what a dangerous problem you have?'

Luke squeezed Theresa's hands and smiled. 'Just because I'm not frightened doesn't mean I don't understand. I'll be very careful, I promise. And I'm very touched by your concern. After the way we parted, so long ago, I was afraid *you* hated me enough to send an exterminator after me. It almost broke my heart that I'd disappointed you so badly, and it didn't help any today to find out that you still hadn't forgiven me.'

Theresa looked down, the soft warmth in Luke's eyes doing strange things to her pulse-rate. 'I did hate you, for a while,' she said, 'but I got over it.' That was about all she seemed to have got over, she thought grimly. Even though she hadn't forgiven him, it gave her no pleasure to know that she had hurt Luke, as she had once thought it would.

'I'm glad.' Luke leaned forward and kissed Theresa lightly on the cheek. 'For old times' sake?' he said, a question in his voice.

'Mmmm,' Theresa murmured non-committally, trying to subdue the surge of floundering emotions that feeling Luke's lips and smelling the clean, woodsy smell of his aftershave rekindled. She pulled her hands free of his and stood up. 'We'd better turn in. It won't be good policy for you to wander around in a daze from lack of sleep. I'll take the top bunk.'

She retreated to the bathroom, changed into her pyjamas, and climbed up into the bunk. A short time later, Luke turned out the lights and got into his bed. All the while, he had been completely silent. Theresa lay facing the wall, her muscles so knotted that she knew she would never be able to sleep. When Luke was silent, she knew, it did not mean that his mind was not working a mile a minute. She could almost feel it working, spinning ideas, thinking through problems in his own unique way. If only he would talk to her, so she could help. But what could she do? She had never felt more helpless.

'Theresa?' came Luke's soft voice. 'Are you asleep?'

'No,' she answered. 'Are you?' She asked the foolish question automatically, then grimaced to herself. She was falling under Luke's spell again, where sensible questions gave way to silliness, and silliness turned into seriousness. She heard Luke chuckle as if he knew what was happening only too well.

'Probably,' he answered. 'It seems like a dream, being here with you. Tell me, Theresa, if this is a dream and we're not on an ordinary train, but a time machine that can go either forwards into the future or backwards in time, which way will you go, and how far?'

'I'm not in the mood for games,' Theresa answered crossly. She was not going to let him entrap her again.

'Then get in the mood.' The velvet voice had a steely edge. 'I want to know the answer.'

Theresa frowned into the darkness. She might as well answer. It was an interesting question. She might go forwards a week or two, even more. Then she would know for certain what was going to happen to Luke. That thought gave her cold shivers. No, not forwards. What she really wished was that she could go back about a week, never have met Josephine McDonald, whose husband's involvement with an exotic dancer in New Orleans was the reason she was on this blasted train, and not be tangled up with Luke Thorndike again.

'Backwards a week,' she answered.

'Hmmm.' Luke cleared his throat. 'You mean that you wish I was in this compartment alone, not knowing that those two men are after me?'

Blast! He'd trapped her into that. 'No! I thought if I went back, you would too,' she said.

'No, you didn't,' Luke contradicted. 'You wish I'd stayed far away and out of your life.'

Hearing him say it so bluntly and perceptively made a sudden ache form in Theresa's chest. Did she really wish that? Not if it meant that harm would come to him. No matter how confused, aggravated and upset he made her, she didn't want him hurt.

'No, I don't, Luke,' she said softly. 'I'm just worried, that's all. Now go to sleep.'

'I'll try,' he answered, 'but only if you promise not to worry. I'll be all right. Promise?'

'Mmmm,' Theresa said, non-committally. That was a promise she knew she couldn't make as long as a threat hung over Luke's life.

'Theresa?' Luke prompted again.

'No, I don't promise!' she snapped. 'I'll worry if I want to, and you can stay awake all night if you want to!'

Luke chuckled. 'Goodnight, Terry, love.'

Theresa scowled into the darkness. Luke probably thought the fact that she was worried about him meant something that it didn't mean at all. She would be worried about anyone whose life was in danger, especially anyone who seemed to take it as lightly as Luke did. She turned on to her stomach, then her side, then on to her back again, trying to find a position in which she could relax. It was impossible. The sheep she tried to count would not jump the fence, but stood still, bleating at her accusingly, 'What are you going to do about Luke?'

What could she do? She was going to get off the train, check in at her hotel, and then begin pursuing the errant Toby McDonald. Or was she? How could she? Gradually she was forced to admit to herself that there was no way in the world she could do that, not knowing all the while where Luke was and whether he was safe. She would imagine all kinds of terrible things. It would drive her crazy. Crazier than being with him did. The 'whys' of both kinds of craziness she did not want to think about right now. She only knew that there was just one answer to her problem. She would have to stick with him like glue until she was sure he would be all right.

'Luke,' she whispered, hanging her head over the side of her bunk, 'are you asleep?'

'I don't think so,' he answered. 'Are you?'

'No, I think I'm delirious,' she replied. 'Tell me, does your apartment really have a spare bedroom?'

CHAPTER TWO

LUKE was silent for so long that Theresa wondered whether he was shocked by her question, or figuratively licking his lips, thinking that she was ready to fall into bed with him again, this time for a real fling. His voice, when he answered, was so flat and noncommittal that she could not tell.

'Yes, it does,' he replied. 'Don't you have a place to stay?'

'Of course I do,' she said impatiently. 'I have a reservation at the Hyatt that I'll have to cancel.'

'I see. But you'd rather stay with me. Why? Do you want my company, or are you only interested in playing watchdog.?'

'Does it matter?' Theresa snapped. If his male ego was going to prevent him from taking advantage of her help, then he could just fend for himself.

'A good question,' Luke replied. After another seemingly interminable pause, he said, 'No, I guess not. But I don't want you hovering over me like a mother hen, nor getting some lame-brained idea that you can keep me locked up. I intend to be out and about whenever I feel like it. If the deadly duo are really after me, I intend to run them ragged, not hole up like some pitiful, cornered animal. Is that clear?'

'Yes, Luke,' Theresa said quickly, relieved that he had not made any further issue of her motivation. She did not want to examine it too closely herself, lest she discover that there was more involved than concern for Luke's life.

'Good girl,' Luke said. Then he chuckled.

'What's the joke?' Theresa asked warily, wondering what outlandish new idea had struck his funny bone.

'I was wondering if I could make the twins a better offer than they've got from Big Joey to stay on my trail so that you would stay with me. I do enjoy your company, you know.'

'Only you would think of that,' Theresa said with a sigh. 'Goodnight, Luke.'

'Goodnight, Terry, love,' he replied, his voice seductively soft. 'Sweet dreams.'

That, Theresa thought grimly, sounded very much like a warning. Well, if Luke thought he could change her mission from one of protection to something more romantic, he could think again. She was not going to let herself get romantically involved with a man she could never marry because she could never trust him. Nor was she up for a fling with him, even though he was no longer married. She wasn't a fling sort of person. He ought to know that. She closed her eyes. He hadn't better try anything...

A hand was shaking her shoulder. 'Wake up, Terry, love.'

Theresa opened her eyes slowly, dragging herself back to consciousness from a deep sleep. 'Don't call me that,' she grumbled crossly, her eyes meeting a pair of dark brown eyes staring over the edge of her bunk. She stared back, watching entranced as Luke's wide mouth curved into a smile that lighted golden sparks in the depths of his eyes. She felt herself smiling back, as if his will had taken possession of her, forcing her to feel warm and happy at the sight of him. That, she decided, was no way to start this day. She was going to have to keep the upper hand over both her emotions and his charm. She looked away, sat up, and rubbed her eyes. 'What time is it?'

'Almost seven-thirty. After you went to the lounge car last night, I signed us up for breakfast at eight. I don't know about you, but I'm starved. I didn't get much dinner last night.' Luke cocked his head and looked at Theresa thoughtfully. 'You could use a little more weight. You're too thin. We ought to be able to take care of that in New Orleans.'

'I am not too thin,' Theresa said, frowning. 'I just don't have the baby fat I did five years ago. Now sit down and let me get out of here. You're in the way.'

'Tch, tch, a morning grouch,' Luke said. He moved away from the ladder to the upper bunk. 'Come on down.'

As soon as Theresa had turned her back and started to lower herself over the side, she felt Luke's hands grasp her about the waist and she was whisked to the floor.

'There you are,' he said, taking advantage of his position to slide his arms around Theresa and pull her against him, her back to his front. She stiffened, holding rigidly still as he leaned his head forward so that his lips grazed her cheek, trying to ignore the wonderful feelings of cosy warmth that being held in his arms provided.

'Let go of me, Luke,' she warned. He paid no attention, instead tightening his grip and rubbing his cheek against hers.

'You know,' he said, 'I really am looking forward to having you staying with me. I think I'll send the fat boys a thank-you note. I know if it weren't for them and your strong sense of professional duty, you wouldn't be. I have no illusions that you really care whether I, personally, am dead or alive. It's the principle of the thing, isn't it?'

Theresa groaned inwardly. Luke was obviously going to keep trying to trick her into admitting that she cared about him, although why he was so persistent she wasn't sure. Probably he'd decided that by now she was fair game for a seduction. She had better set some rules right now.

'Yes, it is,' she answered, 'and I am not interested in any games of "Luke and Terry try out the Three Bears' biggest bed" on the side. If you keep trying to paw me, I'm apt to show you how very good I've become at karate.' When Luke still did not release her, she added, 'Do you have any idea what the first move I make to get out of your hold right now is? I'll give you a clue. It's apt to hurt a certain sensitive area quite a lot.'

Luke removed his arms instantly. 'You wouldn't,' he said accusingly. At Theresa's severe look, he nodded. 'You would. Well, I guess it's a comfort to have that skill protecting me.'

'That,' Theresa said, 'is a better attitude.' She retreated to the bath to dress, feeling as if she'd already been in combat. If she couldn't make herself more immune to the advances she was sure Luke would try in the future, she was going to be exhausted. Why was it that common sense was such a weak force compared to sexual attraction? And why did he have to be the one man in the world who affected her that way?

When Theresa emerged from the bath, dressed in a bright print cotton blouse and skirt in anticipation of the warmth of New Orleans, Luke was lying on his bunk, his eyes closed. She looked at him warily. He was wearing a white buccaneer shirt, and tan trousers in the latest, somewhat baggy, style. With his deep tan and dark, dramatic handsomeness, he still looked more as if he should be in front of the cameras, rather than behind them. His eyelashes were twice as long as any normal man's, fanning out against his cheeks and curling upwards at the ends. His face gave no evidence of stress or fear, the corners of his mouth in their usual upward curve, as if he were always ready to smile. Theresa felt a dangerous tightness in her midsection and looked away.

'I'm ready,' she said.

'So am I,' Luke replied, opening his eyes and holding out his hand towards her. 'Help me up?'

Theresa eyed the hand suspiciously. 'Help yourself,' she said, turning away.

Luke pushed himself from the bunk with a terrible groan. 'My aching back,' he complained, 'and the wretched woman won't even help me up.' He draped an arm around Theresa's shoulders. 'Why is it I have the feeling you don't trust me? Don't you think we'd better trust each other if we're going to vanquish the Dee and Dum threat together? You know perfectly well that I'm not going to assault you. Maybe a little kiss now and then, or a little squeeze, but nothing else. Or is it that you don't trust yourself?'

'If it makes you happy to think so, do,' Theresa snapped, shaking off his arm. 'On the subject of Dee and Dum, in case we see them in the dining car, I should tell you that I led them to believe I'm a secretary, looking for work in New Orleans. For heaven's sake, don't tell them I'm a private investigator. I was holding my breath for an hour last night for fear you'd let that cat out of the bag. It was bad enough that you told them just about everywhere you'd be likely to go. And if they are there, introduce yourself. They already know who you are, but I'd like to find out their names.'

As luck would have it, the twins were nowhere in sight during the time that Theresa and Luke ate their breakfast, but they came wandering in and took seats at another table just as Theresa and Luke were leaving. They nodded, but gave no sign of wanting to converse. Undeterred, Luke stopped at their table.

'I wanted to introduce myself,' he said. 'Don't think we got around to that last night. My name's Luke Thorndike. I'm a screenwriter.' He held out his hand toward the nearest twin, the one in the striped suit.

At first the man appeared reluctant, then he shook Luke's hand. 'Wilber Morton,' he said.

'I'm William,' said the second twin, as Luke held out his hand to him.

'Wilber and William Morton,' Luke said. He took out his perpetually present notebook. 'You don't have a business card I could have, do you?' he asked as he scribbled. 'The reason I ask, is that you two are a rather unique pair, and I think there might be parts for you in the story I'm working on. I'd like to be able to get in touch with you later, if you think you'd like to take a fling at an acting job. It could pay quite well, and be a lot of fun for you besides.'

While Theresa watched, wide-eyed, at this latest example of Luke's inventiveness, the twins stared at each other in surprise.

'Well—er—no, we don't have cards,' Wilber said. 'Actually, we move around quite a lot. Sales, you know.'

'Mmm, yes. I see,' said Luke. He pulled out a little leather case and handed a card to Wilber. 'In that case, you get in touch with me if you think you'd like to try it. Say, in about six months. They should be casting by then.'

Wilber took the card, holding it gingerly at arm's length and staring at it. 'Well—er—thanks, Mr Thorndike,' he said at last. 'We've never done any acting, but we'll talk it over.'

'Good,' said Luke. He smiled cheerfully. 'Have a nice time in New Orleans. Maybe I'll see you around.'

Theresa felt as if she were holding her breath all the way back to Room F. When they were inside, she exploded.

'How can you do that?' she cried. 'I saw it, but I still don't believe it. You acted as if you thought Wilber and William were just two nice little fat men! And how did you ever come up with that wild story on the spur of the moment?'

Luke shrugged. 'I live by invention, remember? Besides, I thought it might be a good idea to give them an alternative to doing me in. Do you think they might take the bait?'

'Very doubtful,' Theresa said, sinking down on to one of the seats, their bunks now having disappeared into the walls for the day. 'Most likely, if they don't do Big Joey's bidding, they'll wind up at the bottom of Lake Michigan wearing little cement shoes.'

'Little cement shoes,' Luke echoed thoughtfully, sitting down opposite Theresa. 'Delightful image that creates. Wilber and William standing there in Neptune's kingdom, watching the fishes swimming by.' He grinned suddenly. 'I hope that doesn't happen to them, because after seeing that odd little pair I've decided to write them into my story. I thought they definitely looked interested in the idea. Are you sure there's no chance they'll take my offer?'

Theresa shook her head, still marvelling at Luke's casual approach to the threat on his life. 'God only knows,' she replied. 'I suppose anything is possible. Just don't bank on it, OK? For instance, if Wilber and William offer to take you for a drive in the park and I'm not there to stop you, don't go with them. It might be your last ride anywhere.'

'Yes, ma'am,' Luke replied. He smiled, his eyes so soft and warm that Theresa could feel their glow across the space between them and feel the answering warmth spreading unbidden into her heart. 'You don't know how much I appreciate your watching over me, Terry, love,' he said. 'I don't think I'd last long without you.'

'Nonsense,' she said tightly. 'I'm not sure how much good I'll be able to do. I'll have to call my brother when we get to your apartment, and see what he recommends. He's a lot more experienced in this type of thing than I am. Which reminds me, I have a job to do in New Orleans myself. Since I'm helping you, I think it's only fair that you help me. I'll take you with me when I have to go out and put you to use asking questions. As clever as you are, you'll probably find out more than I could. Fair enough?'

'I'm at your service,' Luke replied. 'This is sounding like more fun all the time. When do we begin?'

'Tomorrow, I expect,' Theresa replied. 'It's likely the woman Mr McDonald is supposed to be with is in the French Quarter somewhere. At least your apartment will be handier for that. Where did you say it is?'

'On Dumaine Street. It's almost in the middle of the Quarter, as I remember. I haven't seen Harry's apartment, but he always goes first class, so I can imagine it's quite nice. He's an artist, so the décor is apt to be dramatic. He said it's full of plants that I'll have to water, and there's a cat I'm to feed.'

'He wasn't kidding about the plants,' Theresa said, when early that afternoon a taxi deposited them at the venerable but beautifully kept apartment building. There was a small courtyard in front, lush with plants, a tiny fountain goddess sprinkling water into a basin shaped like a seashell in the middle. Every window in every apartment they could see had plants inside and a window-box outside.

Inside, the plant population was even more impressive. The huge, high-ceilinged living-room was painted a stark white, and seemed filled to overflowing with greenery. The only furniture for sitting was a number of immense square cushions covered in various shades of green. Rows of pink azaleas by the French doors relieved the greenness and carried over to more azaleas on the small terrace outside.

'I'm going to feel like part of a tossed salad,' Luke commented. 'Harry must be going through his green period. My God, what an ugly cat.' A gaunt-looking Siamese had come wandering from behind a potted fig tree, yowling an ill-tempered-sounding greeting.

Theresa had been inspecting the back part of the apartment, finding a kitchen that had obviously been recently redone with a fantastic array of new appliances and cabinets.

'Nice kitchen,' she commented to Luke. 'Where are the bedrooms? I only see one other door.'

'Must be here somewhere,' he said cheerfully. He opened the door and then whistled softly. 'Wow! Harry has really been living it up. That is the biggest bed I ever saw. It must be a custom job.'

'Your friend has strange taste,' Theresa commented drily. Strange, she thought, was a moderate word for it. It bordered on kinky. The huge circular bed was covered in pale green satin, with a dozen or more furry scatter pillows scattered around on it. The floor was covered with a thick, white carpet, with several fur rugs lying on top. On the white walls were assorted pictures of nudes in erotic poses. 'And even stranger habits, I'll wager,' she added, pointing to the mirrored ceiling above the bed. 'How well do you know him?'

'Not as well as I thought I did,' Luke replied, his eyes slowly traversing the room. 'This is really something.'

Theresa could see by the half-smile on Luke's face that he was more entertained than appalled by the room. She went to the one remaining door, which opened off the bedroom. It opened into an equally

elaborate bath, with mirrored walls and a jacuzzi tub
that looked big enough for two or three people. There
was, she thought grimly, something funny going on
here. She walked back out of the bedroom and surveyed the rest of the apartment carefully. As she had
begun to suspect, there wasn't a second bedroom.
There wasn't even a sofa in the living-room where a
second person could sleep. And, she would wager,
Luke had known that all along. Well, if he thought
he was going to play that kind of a game, he had a
very large surprise coming. She stood in the middle
of the living-room, her hands planted on her hips,
scowling darkly. That man had done it now. He was
just as untrustworthy as ever. He didn't deserve any
help.

'Luke Thorndike, get out here,' she said loudly.

'That's some bathroom, isn't it?' he asked as he
emerged from the bedroom. 'What's wrong, Terry,
love?' as he spotted her frowning face.

'Wrong? Why, nothing, Luke, darling,' Theresa
said sarcastically. 'Except that there is only one
bedroom here and it looks like something from a
porno flick!' she added in a low roar. 'If you think
I'm still naïve enough to fall for this trick, you are
sadly mistaken. You must have decided that I'm fair
game, now that I'm five years older and you're un-
attached. Well, forget it! And forget having me around
for either company or protection. Hire a talkative
bodyguard instead. That is, if you have sense enough
to know you need one. I'm leaving as soon as I can
find the telephone amid all of this shrubbery and call
a taxi.' She started to look around, expecting Luke to
try and cajole her into staying with one of his flights

of fancy. Instead he snarled back at her in a voice she had never heard before.

'Stand still a minute so I can talk to you,' he ordered. When Theresa had turned to face him, he glared at her, his dark brows almost meeting above his long, straight nose, his face so bleak that she scarcely recognised him. 'You can think what you like, Theresa,' he said, 'but I did think there were two bedrooms here, and I had no idea that the one there is would be ... like it is. Perhaps what Harry said was that the bed was big enough for two rooms. He was pretty potted when we talked about it. However, I had no intention of leading you into temptation. You are doing that yourself, my dear, imagining things that just aren't so, just as you did five years ago. I had hoped you would have gained a little perspective by now, but apparently you are still too naïve to know that the world is not painted in black and white. You're still afraid to look at anything positive, when the negative is so much easier and safer. I'm very sorry about that. You'll never know how sorry.' He pointed toward a small table in front of the french windows. 'There's the telephone.' With that, he wheeled around and walked into the bedroom, banging the door behind him.

Theresa stared after him, a huge lump forming in her throat. She had never seen Luke really angry before, not even when she had been so angry with him that day five years ago. Now he did not want her to stay, and she doubted he would do anything to protect himself from the Morton twins. Feeling almost sick, tears starting to trickle down her cheeks, she went to the telephone, found the number of a taxi company in the directory, and made her call. She picked up her suitcase, started toward the front door, then looked towards the bedroom door. She went to it, raised her hand to knock, and then lowered it again. What could she say? Nothing that would help. She couldn't stay here now. Silently, she went to the front door again and slipped quietly outside.

'Goodbye, Luke,' she whispered, and closed the door behind her.

CHAPTER THREE

THERESA sailed upwards in the glass-enclosed elevator in the towering atrium at the Hyatt, feeling numb from the effort it had taken to keep from bursting into tears while she registered and got her key. No sooner was she in her room than she let out a strangled sob and flung herself on to her bed. What had she done? Why had she done it? Where had she gone wrong? Images of Luke's face, hard and cold and angry, kept rising before her closed eyes. Try as she might, she could not turn it into his usual warm, smiling expression.

'I can't bear it,' she sobbed aloud. 'I can't bear to have him hate me.' It was no use recalling the hurt of years ago or remembering the suspicions that might never go away. Fool that she was, she would give anything now for one warm smile that would wipe away that terrible image of cold, bleak anger that had pierced her heart like a shaft of icy steel. Or did he truly hate her now? What had he been trying to tell her? Usually, he led her into things, like an artist, painting a picture with words. This time he had left her on her own to discover what he meant. The part about seeing things in black and white was fairly obvious, or at least it seemed so. He was saying that her standards for what was right and wrong were too rigid, that she didn't allow for any extenuating circumstances. She saw him only as a mirror of her father,

not as a very different man with a very different life.
As a result, she had jumped to an unfair conclusion.
And, if what he said about what he had believed to
be true about the bedrooms was true, then she had.

'Oh, why am I so stupid?' she moaned, pushing
herself to a sitting position and pulling half a dozen
Kleenex from the box by her bed to mop her tears.
No wonder Luke thought she had no perspective. He
hadn't taken advantage of her five years ago when he
could easily have done so, and he wouldn't now. He
wasn't that kind of a man. She should have learned
that by now, by being out in the world and meeting
other men. Instead, she had kept him categorised as
an evil man who had taken advantage of her youth
and inexperience, afraid to take a second look and
see him for what he was. He was so . . . so very special.
He wasn't like any other man she'd ever met. He was
more fun to be with than anyone else on earth. There
hadn't been a day in the past five years that she hadn't
thought of something they had shared, some funny,
fanciful, imaginative trick with which he had teased
her own imagination and intelligence into flower. And
she had pretended to herself that she hated him—the
easier negative.

'I don't hate him,' she said softly, 'I never really
did.' But had she really loved him? It had been so
intense that one, brief month. *Maybe* she had loved
him. *Maybe* she still did, she wasn't sure. No one else
had ever made her feel the way he did. He must feel
something for her, too; he had been so angry. *Maybe*
that was the reason he had said he was sorry that she
had no perspective. *Maybe* that was why he had stayed
away from her for so long. He thought she was a

hopeless case. Now, seeing her again, he still liked her and thought *maybe* she had changed. There were so many 'maybes'. Too many. She had to sort them out, find out what she...and Luke...really felt. If she could. He had said she would never know how sorry he was. Did he really mean never? Had he truly written her off now as hopeless? Well, he was wrong about that if he had. She might be a slow learner, but she wasn't hopeless. She was catching on a lot faster now, while he hadn't yet seemed to understand the danger he was in.

The thought of that problem brought another convulsive sob from Theresa's throat, but she dashed away her tears with an impatient hand. She didn't have time to cry any longer. She would die if anything happened to Luke because of her stupidity. It was time to call Quentin and see what advice he could give her. Then she'd decide what to do.

'Do you know anything about a short, fat pair of twins named Wilber and William Morton?' she asked as soon as she had her brother on the phone.

'Wilber and William Morton,' her brother repeated in his slow, methodical voice. 'That's one of the Brimstone brothers' aliases. They're a couple of minor-league racketeers. Last I heard they were in Joliet prison, but they may be out by now. Why?'

'Did you ever hear of them doing any...any hired killings?'

'No. Why?'

Theresa explained what she had heard on the train, and her subsequent attempts to convince Luke he was in danger.

'I suppose it's possible that the Brimstones have decided to move up in the underworld,' Quentin replied, 'but I can't imagine Scarcelli hiring that pair. He has his own troops that are a lot more professional than they are. But still, it isn't something to take lightly. What's the matter with Thorndike? I remember you said he was kind of crazy. He can be kind of dead if he isn't careful.'

'He isn't crazy, he's just . . . imaginative,' Theresa said. 'I like him. Meeting him again, I've discovered . . . well, never mind. I'll tell you later. What shall I do? Contact the local authorities?'

'You can. They can pick the Brimstones up for questioning, but they probably have stories prepared as to why they're in New Orleans and they'll just deny having made any threats. What effect it will have for them to know someone knows why they're really in town is a good question. They might panic and do something in a hurry. They're not the smartest pair in the world. Or they might disappear for a while and come back when they think they've been forgotten, which means Thorndike would have to be on his guard for God knows how long.'

'That sounds like it would be better if they didn't know we're on to them,' Theresa said. 'Any suggestions as to how I can get them to do something nonfatal and get them locked up again?'

'What do you mean, you?' Quentin asked sharply. 'Has Thorndike hired you to protect him? You're not equipped for that kind of a job.'

'No, he hasn't hired me. I just don't want anything to happen to him,' Theresa replied. 'And don't tell me I'm not equipped, or try to play big brother and forbid me to do it, because I'm going to do it anyway.'

Quentin growled something about stubborn sisters, then said pointedly, 'Unless I'm mistaken, you have another case to work on. You do have a responsibility to Mrs McDonald, you know.'

'Don't worry, I'll take care of that, too. How about answering my first question?'

'There's not much you can do unless they make a move. Then it's all apt to happen pretty fast. The best thing would be for Thorndike to pay Scarcelli what he owes him and get him to call off his hit, if that's what it really is about. Somehow, that still doesn't sound quite right to me. Do you want me to see what I can find out?'

'Yes, please do,' Theresa replied. 'Meanwhile, I guess I'll just have to play it by ear. By the way, I'm going to be staying with Luke. I'll let you know the phone number tomorrow.'

'You're going to *what*?'

'You heard me. 'Bye, Quent.'

Theresa dropped the receiver on to its cradle, grabbed her suitcase, and went out of the door. She hadn't consciously decided to go back to Luke's, but as she talked to Quentin she knew there was no other choice. If Luke wouldn't let her in . . . well, she would cross that bridge when she got to it. In a few minutes she had checked out and the doorman had got her a taxi.

'Take me somewhere where I can get a folding bed,' she told the driver. 'You know, the kind with a little foam cushion that people lie out in the sun on. I'm staying with a friend and I don't want to have to sleep on the sofa. It's expensive and lumpy.'

'Sure, I can do that. I think the discount store has them on sale,' the driver replied. He grinned at Theresa in the rear-view mirror. 'Nice guest. I wish my mother-in-law was that thoughtful. She takes my bed.'

'I wouldn't do that,' Theresa replied. Wild horses couldn't get her to sleep in that even wilder bedroom. She was going to try to get over being so uptight, try not to be suspicious of Luke's intentions, but that was going a bit far. Even five years ago, before she knew Luke was married and when her desire for him was almost boundless, she would have run like a deer if he'd led her into a room like that one.

An hour later, the taxi deposited Theresa in front of Luke's apartment. After three stops, she had found what she wanted. The bed was small and light, folded easily, and had a little carrying handle at the top. She stood on the doorstep, clutching her bag in one hand and the bed in the other, suddenly immobilised with fear. Would Luke let her in? What if he had gone out? It was almost dinner time. Finally she set the bed down, banged on the door, and then picked the bed up again. If she had to, she'd knock him down to get inside. Finally, after a second loud knock at the door, Luke answered. Theresa could only stare at him, shocked. He looked tired and haggard, his face drawn and tense. His eyes were red, as if he, too, had been crying. He blinked several times, and gradually his face relaxed into softer lines. After what seemed to Theresa like an eternity, during which her stomach tied itself into an impossible knot, he looked down at the bed she was carrying.

'I don't think I'm buying any of those, ma'am,' he said huskily.

The knot in Theresa's stomach magically untied itself and her knees went weak with relief. Luke didn't hate her, after all.

'I'm giving this one away, sir,' she said. 'I come with it.'

'Well, in that case...' he flung the door wide and bowed gallantly, 'do come in, pretty lady.'

Theresa entered and set down her burdens. 'I thought maybe... *Gesundheit!*' as Luke sneezed violently. 'I thought maybe we could rearrange some plants to sort of wall off part of this room for my bed,' she said, voicing an idea which had come to her as she and the taxi driver had talked. *'Gesundheit!'* as Luke sneezed again.

'I'm allergic to cats,' he explained, blowing his nose, 'and I don't seem to have brought my antihistamine. I was about to go out and get some before my eyes swell shut. Lucky you caught me before I left. After that I was going to go and drown my sorrows for a few hours just like those stupid Earthlings do. Glad you saved me from that. I would have felt even worse tomorrow.'

He smiled, and Theresa realised that he was trying to tell her, obliquely, that he had been sorry she left and was glad she was back. Thank goodness he hadn't been crying his eyes out, as she had first feared. She wouldn't know what to make of that if he had, whether it meant he cared a great deal about her or was really terrified by the threat on his life.

'So am I,' she agreed. 'I have some antihistamines in my suitcase, too, so you're really in luck.' She perched her suitcase on a pile of cushions, opened it, and handed him the bottle. 'I talked to my brother,' she went on. 'He says the Mortons are for real. Their real name is Brimstone, and they're known as minor-league criminals, not killers so far. He says their threat should be taken seriously, anyway, but he seemed to think Scarcelli would have used one of his own men. Is there anyone else you can think of who might have hired them? Anyone in Chicago, for instance?' While she had been talking, she had followed Luke into the kitchen, where he downed a pill with some water and then splashed cold water on his face.

'Lord, my eyes itch,' he said, towelling his face dry. 'No, Terry, love, I don't know anyone else, but that doesn't mean there isn't someone. Success breeds enemies. Maybe there's some poor benighted soul out there who thinks I stole his plot and got famous while he's labouring in obscurity in a nuts and bolts factory. He's been saving up for years just so he could hire old fire and Brimstone to come after me.'

'I guess it's some comfort that they aren't experienced killers,' Theresa said with a sigh.

'Unless they decide to shoot me across a crowded room and hit two or three innocent bystanders instead,' Luke said drily. Then he chuckled. 'Remember that old song?' He began to sing. 'Some enchanted evening, you will see a hit man...'

'Stop that!' Theresa said, then burst into helpless giggles as Luke continued his parody. 'That,' she scolded when he was through, 'was worse than having to listen to Nero fiddle while Rome burned. Quentin wanted to know if you were crazy when I told him you didn't take the Brimstones' threat seriously.'

'And what did you tell him?' Luke asked, suddenly serious.

'Never you mind,' Theresa replied, wrinkling her nose at him. Then, seeing that Luke looked really concerned, she added, 'Of course I don't think you're crazy. I told him you were imaginative.'

'Which sometimes looks very much the same,' Luke said. 'I know. I guess laughing is my way of dealing with tension. I'd a hell of a lot rather die laughing than any other way, given that I'd rather not die at all, ever. Wouldn't you?'

Theresa looked into Luke's eyes, which were searching hers so seriously now. He had such a remarkable way of switching from humour to seriousness in a flash. It was like being on a roller-coaster: exhilarating, and yet sometimes frightening. If you didn't stay with him, you were lost.

'Yes,' she answered his question. 'But I don't think I'm as good at it as you are.'

'You'll learn,' Luke said. He laid his hand on her cheek, and his eyes drifted to her lips.

Theresa held very still, afraid to move lest she send some signal that she did not intend, especially since she was trembling inside from the inner conflict that set in as soon as he touched her. She wanted him to kiss her, and yet she was still afraid. Afraid of the surging emotions that might overwhelm her ability to think. She needed to be able to think clearly as long as Luke's life was in danger, and after that to be able to decide if she dared to love him, with all that might imply.

Then, suddenly, he withdrew his hand, closed his eyes, and shook his head. 'No,' he said, as if to himself. Then he opened his eyes and looked at Theresa again. 'I promised myself not to touch you if you came back. I don't want to frighten you away again. I apologise for being so abrupt before. It was just that . . .' He broke off and made a wry face.

'That's OK,' Theresa said quickly, putting her hand on his arm. 'I understand.'

'Maybe,' Luke said. 'Maybe you do.' Then he shook off his serious mood with a broad grin. 'Right now, see if you can understand why I have a sudden uncontrollable yen for a dozen oysters on the half-shell.'

'You're pregnant?' Theresa suggested, delighted when Luke roared with laughter.

'Not this month,' he joked back. 'I'm sure of it. No, I get this feeling every now and then. I think it has something to do with the way the phase of the moon relates to my home planet. Let us stroll out into the Quarter and find a café with plenty of oysters before I go berserk.'

'Don't forget to keep an eye out for the Brimstone brothers,' Theresa reminded him as they went out the door. 'You're taller and can see a lot better in a crowd than I can.'

'Is that a fact?' Luke said, pretending to be very surprised. 'I always thought you short people made up for it by being able to see through people.'

'Don't I wish?' Theresa replied with a sigh. She wished she could even figuratively see through Luke, so that she could tell just how concerned he really was. She was beginning to feel strongly that he was a lot more worried than he let on. She was less sure of it when, as they began elbowing their way through the inevitable crowd on Bourbon Street, he suddenly took a tight hold on her arm.

'I just saw Dee and Dum,' he said. 'They went into a show that advertises "Fifteen Lovelies Bare It All In Sensuous, Exotic Dances". Shall we follow them and see if it's something their mother would approve of?'

Theresa gave him a disgusted look. 'No. Pretend I'm your mother. I don't let my boys go into shows like that until they're over forty.' Then she suddenly remembered Toby McDonald. 'Darn!' she said, stopping in the middle of the street.

'What's the matter?' Luke asked.

'The man I'm looking for. Toby McDonald. His lady love is supposedly an exotic dancer named Carmelita. We'll probably have to go into that place and see if they know her. But not now!' she added as Luke's eyebrows shot up and he pretended great delight at her announcement. 'Oysters now,' she said firmly.

'Oysters now, dancers later. Sounds good to me,' Luke said. 'Come on.' He took Theresa's arm and propelled her rapidly down Bourbon Street. 'We'll window shop on the way back,' he said, as she dragged on his arm to point out a display of Mardi Gras masks. 'Let's eat while we know where the boys are.'

So he is worried, Theresa thought, reversing her opinion again and hurrying along at his side. She had better stop letting his bravado deceive her.

They turned down Iberville, and soon were entering a brightly lit restaurant where, at a long counter, oyster shuckers were hard at work trying to keep up with the demand, while a crowd milled about, drinking beer and waiting for vacant tables.

'I hope we don't have to wait too long,' Theresa remarked, after Luke had given his name to the head waiter and brought them each a cold beer.

Luke shrugged. 'I'm not worried. Being close to so many oysters makes me feel secure.' Seeing Theresa's anxious expression, he smiled. 'Let's not think about the Brimstones for a while. If I devote much of my mental power to thinking about that pair it will take all of the pleasure out of life and I might as well be dead.'

'All right,' Theresa agreed. 'I've noticed that there are several ladies in here who look as if they'd love to bring some pleasure into your life. There's a blonde over by the wall who hasn't taken her eyes off of you since we came in.' In fact, she mused, being trained to observe such things was not terribly helpful at times. It had taken her only a few seconds to notice that most of the women in the restaurant zeroed in on Luke's handsome face, some of them gawking unashamedly.

'You can't be jealous,' Luke said, his eyebrows raised in exaggerated shock.

'Of course not,' Theresa denied quickly. 'I automatically observe which people react to which other people. You can sometimes discover connections you didn't know about just by watching people's eyes in a crowd. The way she was staring, I wondered if you knew her, or she knew who you are.' And I was wondering how far I could throw her, she added grimly to herself. If that was being jealous, she certainly was, but she was definitely not going to admit it to Luke, even if she had to break their old rule about always telling the truth. Not that she thought they were still playing by those rules, the way Luke was dodging around admitting to his fear of the Brimstones.

Luke flicked a glance toward the blonde, then looked back at Theresa, one eyebrow cocked mischievously. 'Not bad,' he said. 'It's a good thing you're not jealous. I don't know her, but I wouldn't mind meeting her.' He burst out laughing as Theresa glared at him. 'Terry, love, you're turning green. It's not your best colour. Besides, with all of that green in the apartment, I don't think I can stand it.'

'You're imagining things,' Theresa replied tightly. 'I'm simply trying to do my job.'

'Of course,' Luke said, nodding seriously. 'And I'm trying to do mine.'

Theresa frowned. 'What job is that? Annoying me?'

'No, Theresa,' Luke said with a sigh. 'That isn't it. But I guess I should look on the bright side. When you figure that out, my job will be finished.'

'Are you trying to tell me I'm dense?' Theresa demanded, perplexed. Luke's statement made no sense at all to her.

'I don't think dense is quite the word,' he replied. 'Although a kind of apparent denseness can be the result. Ah, our table is ready. Oysters, here I come.'

Although Theresa tried several times during their dinner of oysters, followed by blackened redfish, to get Luke to tell her what the right word would be, he flatly refused, leaving her more confused than ever.

'I already gave you the word, or words, earlier today,' he said. 'You'll have to figure it out for yourself. If I tell you, you'll only deny it.'

That, Theresa thought, was not much help. Luke had inundated her with words. 'Have fun being cryptic,' she said crossly. 'It will probably take me years to unravel what you're driving at.'

'I don't think so,' Luke said. He reached across the table and took hold of Theresa's hand. 'Don't fret about it,' he said gently. 'I think it will come to you suddenly, quite soon. It's that sort of a thing.'

Theresa looked into the warmth of Luke's beautiful, dark eyes, and then down at his hand, enclosing hers. If he meant that his job was to get her to admit to herself that she cared enough about him to be jealous, that job was already done. If he meant that he wanted her to admit it to him, that was something else again, something that might take quite a long time. She would have to be sure she could trust him first, if she ever could. Making jokes about meeting blondes was not very conducive to that kind of trust...especially when she wasn't sure they were jokes.

'Dessert?' suggested the waiter, appearing by their table. 'Cheesecake? Pecan pie?'

'Pecan pie, by all means,' Luke replied instantly.

The waiter looked questioningly at Theresa.

'Oh, I couldn't...' she began, biting her lip. There was nothing she liked better than pecan pie, one of the south's most famous and calorie-laden temptations.

'Yes, she could,' Luke said. 'Two pecan pies.' He grinned at Theresa's scowl. 'Don't let the Earthlings trap you into their bad habits. Perpetual self-denial is deadly, not virtuous. Here we are, enjoying one of the few things they occasionally do really well, producing excellent food. Take advantage of it. One piece of pecan pie won't do any harm. It will only put two ounces on those skinny bones of yours.'

Theresa sighed. She had known being with Luke would not be easy. 'It's not just tonight's pecan pie I'm worried about,' she grumbled. 'It's tomorrow's and the day after that's. I can't really enjoy something that's so fattening.'

'Theresa, that's pitiful!' Luke exclaimed. 'If I thought that was really true, I'd get up and leave this instant.' Then he snapped his fingers and shook his head. 'No, I know it isn't true, and I can't leave. I have my job to do.'

'That job again! First you get me confused. Now you're trying to make me fat. Fat and confused. Is that the way you want me to be? I'm afraid I won't be able to save you from the Brimstone brothers in that condition.'

'Theresa,' Luke said seriously, leaning toward her and peering intently into her eyes, 'I am trying to save you from something far worse than the Brimstone brothers.' His eyes suddenly sparkled with mirth. 'Just doing my job, ma'am,' he said.

'If you don't stop talking about some mysterious job you're doing to or for me, I'm going to throw my pecan pie at you,' Theresa warned. 'I am perfectly happy the way I am. I don't need rearranging.'

Luke leaned back again and lifted one eyebrow. 'Perfectly happy?' he said. 'Really?'

'Yes, really!' Theresa snapped. She glowered at the piece of pie which the waiter now set before her. She ought to show that arrogant Luke Thorndike. She should just let the pie sit there. But...her mouth watered, and she picked up her fork. Maybe one bite. The first taste told her that one bite was impossible. It was heavenly. She slowly ate the pie, afraid to look at Luke and see his triumphant, I-told-you-so expression. She was downing the very last crumb, when she felt a prickling sensation at the nape of her neck. Something was wrong. She raised her head slowly, her face carefully blank. Then she smiled brightly at Luke and leaned towards him as if he had her undivided attention.

'Don't look now,' she said, 'but our mutual friends have arrived. They're taking a table between us and the door. One of them just noticed you, and now they're both looking this way. It was nice of you to tell them about this place.'

'What do we do now?' Luke asked, leaning toward her. 'Do we leap out the window and run like the devil? Is it time for the chase scene? I'll bet those fat fellows can't keep up with us. Can't you picture them huffing and puffing along like the two engines that couldn't, their arms pumping like pistons, getting so hot that smoke pours out of their ears?'

'Oh, Luke, do be serious,' Theresa said, laughing helplessly at the image he had created. 'No, it isn't time for the chase scene. I hope it never is. The thing for us to do is leave calmly, as if nothing were wrong. Then we'll have to keep a sharp eye out to see if they stay for dinner, or start to follow us. If they follow, we'll have to try to get home without ending up in any dark, quiet place where we're alone.'

'That shouldn't be difficult, given the crowds,' Luke said, 'except for the last block before the apartment. Shall we stop and say hello on our way out?'

'If you feel up to it,' Theresa replied. 'I wouldn't mind getting a close look at them to see if I can tell if they're armed.'

'Oh, they have arms all right,' Luke said quickly. 'I shook hands with them. Remember?'

'Ha, ha,' Theresa said, making a face. 'Shall we go?'

'If that's the best laugh I can get, we might as well,' Luke said. 'We'll stop and say hello. Don't want to appear unfriendly.'

Luke greeted the Brimstones jovially, recommended the oysters and redfish, and then bent to whisper something in William's ear which made him look first startled and then burst into hearty laughter.

'What did you tell him?' Theresa demanded, once they were outside.

'A little joke I know about exotic dancers,' Luke replied with a grin. 'Made quite a hit, didn't it? Also lets them know how easy they are for me to spot. I thought that might be a good idea.'

'So they can be more careful in the future?' Theresa asked sarcastically. 'It might interest you to know that either Wilber has an extra roll of fat, or he's got a shoulder holster on. I suggest we get back to your apartment as quickly as possible.'

'They won't try anything in this crowd,' Luke said, as they once again turned down Bourbon Street. 'Besides, they may not be following us.'

He strolled along at what, to Theresa, was an aggravatingly slow pace. Then, to her consternation, he stopped to watch a juggler performing on a street corner.

'Luke,' she said, tugging at his sleeve, 'we ought to keep moving.' He ignored her. When she tugged again, he looked down.

'Have you ever wondered,' he asked seriously, 'what it would be like if everyone could do everything well? If we could all juggle, or do magic, or play the trumpet? Would anyone watch?' He returned his attention to the juggler, applauding enthusiastically when the young man managed to keep five oranges in the air with his hands, and a plate spinning on his head at the same time.

Theresa, instead, watched Luke. He was watching the young juggler intently, his mouth curved in an admiring smile, as if it were the most wonderful sight he had ever seen. Theresa sighed. Luke wasn't stupid or foolish, he was simply entranced by life. And she, she thought, as a warm but anxious feeling invaded her heart, was entranced by him. It was a dangerous situation, for both of them. If only she were tall enough to see over the crowd, to see if the Brimstone brothers were on their trail, she would feel a little better. She took hold of Luke's arm and squeezed it hard. He looked at her again, eyebrows raised questioningly.

'Would you mind taking a look around for the twins?' she asked.

'That's better,' Luke said, his eyes twinkling mischievously. He turned around, looking in all directions, then bent so that his face was level with Theresa's. 'You really can't see much from down here, can you?' he commented.

'No,' Theresa said, frowning. 'What did you mean by "that's better"?'

'I told you that I didn't want you playing mother hen, and I meant it. You may ask me to be careful, but don't start ordering me around or pulling on me. Understood?' His eyes searched Theresa's from only inches away.

'Yes, Luke,' Theresa said with a sigh. As if it wasn't difficult enough to try to protect him, without him being stubborn! 'Did you see anything when you were up in the clouds?'

'No,' he replied. 'We seem to be alone with only a few thousand other friendly people.' He suddenly leaned forward and kissed Theresa's lips, holding his lips against hers for several seconds. Then he pulled back, shaking his head and smiling ruefully. 'I don't know what made me do that. It must have been the oysters. I hope you're not offended.'

'Offended?' Theresa said weakly. It felt as if a lightning bolt had grazed her lips, leaving her scarred and shaken as a tree on a hilltop. She tried to get her mind to work, but it seemed all scrambled. Had it felt like that before, when he'd kissed her? She couldn't remember it being quite like that. Maybe it was only because she was nervous about the Brimstones. She should be nervous about that. So should Luke. But she didn't feel nervous, only excited. They shouldn't be standing here for too long, she knew that, even if Luke hadn't seen anything, but at the moment she didn't seem to care. Finally, she partially roused herself. 'No. But I do think...that is, would you mind if we...'

She floundered to a stop, aware that Luke's face was still so close that she would only have to move a few inches to kiss him back and find out if the lightning happened again. His lips were so soft and warm-looking, his eyes so beautiful and glowing... Gravity alone seemed responsible for the way that she swayed forwards until her lips again touched his.

'Oh!' she said breathlessly, moving back a little, her eyes still open wide. It had happened again! She closed her eyes and swayed forwards a second time. This time she felt Luke's arms close around her, and they were locked in an embrace that sent her soaring, her mouth opening to the hungry assault from Luke's tongue, completely unaware of the milling crowd around them until loud and continuing applause reminded her of the juggler and where they were. This was insane! She had forgotten all about the Brimstones!

With a quick move she pushed herself free and looked around her, only to see a circle of people around them, smiling and applauding. Her cheeks flaming, she stared up at Luke. He grinned down at her, his eyes alight with devilish mischief.

'They seem to think we do that quite well,' he said, giving a little bow to the crowd, who applauded again. 'Shall we do it again down the street a ways? We might develop quite a following.'

'Certainly not!' Theresa said, scowling. 'I take back what I said earlier. You are definitely crazy!' She turned and marched stiffly away down the street. If Luke wanted to follow her, fine. If he didn't, it was just too bad. She couldn't possibly protect a man who had no more common sense than a gnat! He was absolutely infuriating. Of course, she had kissed him back, but he was the one who had started it. And if he hadn't grabbed her like that...

A rough-looking man bumped into Theresa and pushed by her. She felt a tug on the strap of her shoulder-bag. That did it! All she needed now was to be robbed! She ducked, whirled, and lifted as smoothly as a textbook manoeuvre. Then she turned and let out a horrified gasp, her eyes glued open in unblinking agony. It was not some ugly stranger, it was Luke flying through the air. He landed on the pavement with a thud, and then lay there, perfectly still.

'Boy, lady, you don't fool around,' said a teenage boy, grinning at her admiringly.

'Oh, shut up and call an ambulance!' Theresa cried, dropping to her knees beside Luke. She put her hand on his forehead and brushed his hair back, tears pouring down her cheeks. 'Luke, speak to me. Please, Luke. *Please*. Say something.'

CHAPTER FOUR

LUKE opened his eyes and slowly focused them on Theresa's face. 'Does it have to be brilliant?' he asked. He pushed himself to a sitting position and rubbed his head. 'I guess I'm all here.'

'Oh, Luke, I'm so sorry,' Theresa sobbed. 'I thought you were stealing my bag. I mean, I thought someone was. I didn't know it was you.'

'So I deduced, somewhere in mid-air,' Luke said drily, 'when I realised you couldn't have known it was me.'

The teenage boy reappeared with a policeman in tow. 'What's going on here?' demanded the policeman.

'He tried to steal her bag,' the boy said, pointing at Luke.

Theresa got to her feet. 'No, he didn't,' she said. 'It was a mistake. He's a friend of mine. But this big, rough-looking man had just bumped into me and I thought...Luke, be careful,' she said, taking his hand as he struggled to his feet.

'I'm all right,' Luke said gruffly, scowling at Theresa and brushing at his clothing. 'Don't fuss.'

Men! How they hated to admit they were hurt, Theresa thought. The policeman was frowning at her, too.

'You ought to be more careful if you're that good at self-defence,' he said. 'You could really hurt someone.'

'I know,' Theresa said, feeling suddenly very small and stupid. 'I've never done anything like that before.'

'Could I see some identification?' the policeman asked. He gave her a lop-sided smile. 'I like to keep track of all of the lethal weapons in the Quarter.'

'Of course.' Theresa felt for her bag. It was not hanging from her shoulder! 'It's gone! Now it's really gone,' she said, looking frantically around on the street where Luke had fallen. 'It must have happened when I was kneeling beside you,' she said to Luke. 'I was so worried, I didn't even notice.' Tears of anger welled in her eyes, making her more miserable than ever. 'This is awful!' she said, stamping her foot in frustration. 'This is turning into a nightmare!'

'Calm down, Terry, love,' Luke said softly, putting his arm around her shoulders. 'Nothing irreparable has happened.' He pulled his wallet from inside his shirt and handed it to the officer. 'I'm Luke Thorndike,' he said, 'and this is Theresa Long. I've known her for many years, and I'll vouch for the fact that she is, generally, an upstanding citizen.'

'You from California, too?' the policeman asked Theresa as he handed Luke's identification back.

'No, Chicago,' she replied. 'I work for my brother's detective agency, which is how I happen to know self-defence.'

The policemen persisted with his questions until he had found out why Theresa was in town and where she was staying.

'At least I know she'll be safe,' he commented, winking broadly at Luke. 'Well, if your bag shows up, we'll call, and if I turn up anything on McDonald, I'll let you know.' He gave Theresa a friendly salute and walked away.

Theresa looked up at Luke and grimaced wryly. 'I don't blame you if you're mad at me,' she said. 'I'm mad at myself. I'm so stupid, it's pitiful. I probably deserve to lose my bag. I knew I shouldn't have splurged on a Gucci. How does your head feel? Are you hurt anywhere else?'

Luke chuckled. 'Terry, love,' he said, 'my head doesn't ache, so I think all I'll have is a bump for a day or two. Everything else is fine, and I'm not angry with you. This has been one of the most memorable evenings I've ever spent. Maybe the most memorable. But I think it's time to call it a night. Shall we head for home before any more excitement breaks out? Or shall we hang around and see if we can get the Brimstones to follow us?'

'Good lord, no,' Theresa said with feeling. 'Let's get out of here.' She was more than glad to have Luke tuck his arm around her as they started down the street. Somehow, she felt that she needed protection as much as he did, most likely from herself. They had gone only a short distance when she stopped. At Luke's questioning look she said, 'That's funny. I thought I heard someone calling my name.'

Luke turned his head and listened intently. Then he turned around to look.

'For God's sake,' he said, a grin spreading across his face, 'look what's coming. Two Boy Scouts doing their good deed for the day.'

Theresa stood on tiptoe. 'Oh, my goodness!' she said. 'I don't believe this.'

Coming toward them at a trot, looking for all the world like round, puffing engines, came the Brimstone brothers. Wilber, in the lead, was clutching Theresa's bag.

'Miss Long,' he panted, 'thank goodness we found you! Hello, Thorndike.' He held the bag out to Theresa. 'We saw this fellow duck into a doorway about two blocks back with this bag in his hands. William said it looked like yours. It's a real Gucci, isn't it? I thought so. Anyway we—er—pursuaded the fellow to hand it over, and we checked the identification. Sure glad we got it back for you.'

'So am I,' Theresa said, her eyes still wide in amazement. 'I don't know how to thank you. I thought it was surely gone forever.'

'No thanks necessary,' Wilber said gallantly. 'Glad to be of help. A person needs all the help they can get these days, with all the crooks there are around. But I guess you'd know about that. We were kind of surprised to find out you're a private detective. Thought you said you were a secretary.'

'I usually say that,' Theresa said quickly. 'Private investigator tends to intimidate some people, and others ask too many questions.'

'I can believe that,' William said. 'You folks going this way? We were about to head back to our room. Been a long day.'

With that, the twins fell into step with Luke and Theresa, chatting amiably until Luke and Theresa turned off on Dumaine Street.

'This day is getting curiouser and curiouser, as Alice would have said,' Theresa commented as they started down the much quieter street. 'I wouldn't have bet a penny that those two would give back my bag if they did find it.'

'Neither would I,' Luke agreed. Suddenly his grip on Theresa tightened and he pulled her into a dark, recessed doorway.

'What . . .' she began, but he put his hand over her mouth.

'Just in case they were trying to lull us into a false sense of security,' he whispered, 'I think we'll stay here for a few minutes. OK?'

Theresa nodded, a feeling of despair sweeping over her. She should have thought of that, but she hadn't. Tears tried to well up again, but she blinked them back. A blubbering idiot was the last thing Luke needed on his hands. She not only wasn't any help, she was positively dangerous to him! He'd be better off without her. She stood silently in the circle of his arm, trying to be alert and watchful, but finding it difficult to fight off the dreamy feeling that being so close to Luke produced. She wanted to put her arms around him and lean against him and forget everything but this tiny little dark world of a doorway in New Orleans where they were alone together. Instead she held herself rigid, until at last Luke looked at his watch and nodded.

'Ten minutes,' he said. 'I think if they were coming back, they would have by now, don't you?'

'I think so,' Theresa agreed. She watched as Luke leaned his head out and surveyed the street.

'All clear,' he announced. 'Let's move.' He grinned suddenly. 'Is that the right thing to say, under the circumstances? I still feel as if I'm playing cops and robbers.'

'It will do just fine,' Theresa said, hanging on to Luke's hand as he took off at a trot down the street. Any way he wanted to play it was fine. He was doing a lot better than she was.

In a few minutes, they were back inside the apartment. Luke looked at his watch again.

'Four minutes from that doorway,' he announced. 'We could probably do it faster.'

'You could do it faster without me,' Theresa said. She tossed her bag on to the floor and flopped face down on a huge green cushion. 'In fact, I think you'd get along a lot better without me,' she mumbled. 'I'll get out of your way tomorrow, and go back to chasing Toby McDonald. Maybe I can do that right.'

'Move over,' Luke said, lowering himself on to the cushion. He propped himself on one elbow and frowned at Theresa. 'What do you mean, get out of my way? You're not thinking of leaving again, are you?'

Theresa flicked a teary-eyed glance at him and nodded.

'You're going to leave me to face those two all alone?' he demanded.

'I think you'd be better off,' Theresà replied, swallowing hard, afraid to look into those beautiful dark eyes that were staring at her so accusingly. 'I'm t-trying to think of your welfare.' She flinched as Luke laid a hand against her cheek, then turned her face towards him. For a moment he continued staring at her.

'Turn over on your back,' he said finally, 'and look around. What do you see?'

Only briefly, Theresa thought of saying that she did not feel like playing one of Luke's games. Before the thought could reach her tongue, she quelled it. This was no time for a petty argument. She turned over and looked.

'I see fig trees and palm trees and hanging baskets of begonias and some ferns . . . and what I always call airplane plants, with the little ones flying around the big ones, and a Norfolk pine.' She looked over at Luke. 'Is that what you mean?'

Luke nodded. 'It's a regular jungle, isn't it? And here we are, on this little green island in the middle of it, lost to the rest of civilisation. For all we know, they may never find us. The crocodiles in that swamp below us may get us. The lean panther that stalks the jungle may attack. But I'm not afraid, because I have you to talk to and to be brave for. If I were alone, I doubt I'd last a day. I'd be frightened and foolish and fall into the swamp and the crocodiles would eat me.' He smiled crookedly. 'You don't want the crocodiles to eat me, do you?'

Theresa shook her head. 'No,' she said slowly. She turned on her side and faced him. 'Why did you make up that story, instead of just telling me you wanted me to stay so you wouldn't be alone?' she asked.

'I don't know,' Luke said. 'Maybe because it's easier for me. I'm too used to living among Earthlings. It isn't permitted for males of the species to admit to being afraid, in spite of the fact that only fools never are. And I think it makes it easier for you, too. Does it? Or would you prefer I just be blunt?'

'No,' Theresa answered. 'I think you're right, in a way. It is easier, and much more fun.' But in another way, he wasn't right. Nothing was any easier now. For, as she had watched his face and listened to his voice as he'd woven his little story, an almost unbearable ache had built inside her. She knew she never wanted to be far from that voice, never far from the sight of his face. She loved Luke Thorndike so much that it hurt. How much more would it hurt her to love him? What did his wanting her to stay really mean? Did she dare to begin to hope that he cared for her?

'Well,' Luke said, 'will you stay?'

'I already said I didn't want the crocodiles to get you, didn't I?' Theresa replied with a rueful smile. 'Just be careful you don't trip over me and fall into the swamp.'

'Or come up behind you suddenly and have you throw me in,' Luke teased. 'Maybe I'd better learn some counter-measures.'

'If you hadn't kissed me like that, with all of those people around...' Theresa stopped, blushing. The kiss had been as much her fault as Luke's, and the look he was giving her said only too plainly that she had better not try and pin the blame on him.

'That's better,' Luke said, giving the tip of her nose a playful tap with his finger. 'For some mystical reason, we both knew it was time for that kiss, and I, for one, don't regret it at all. I was rather surprised, though, at the response we got. With all of the outlandish goings-on on Bourbon Street, I didn't think anyone would notice. I guess that proves an out-

standing performance will draw a crowd every time.'
He stood up and held out a hand to Theresa. 'Maybe
if we practise, we can get even better.'

Theresa eyed his hand suspiciously and then started
to push herself up without touching it. She was definitely not ready for another kiss just yet, not that
ready to trust Luke not to take advantage of her obvious response to him. She gave a startled, 'Oh!' when
Luke roughly pushed her back down on the cushion.

'Take my hand,' he said firmly, holding it out again.
'I can't wait forever for you to figure out that I am
not a seething mass of corrupt intentions. I only
wanted to help you up.'

Avoiding meeting Luke's eyes, Theresa took his
hand and let him pull her to her feet. She felt wobbly
and exhausted from the emotional turmoil of the day,
his hand strong and warm and firm. Trustworthy. The
hand of someone who would always be there. But her
father's hand had felt like that, too, when she was
little. She sighed heavily as Luke released his grip.
Would that spectre always be there?

'What's wrong, Terry, love?' Luke asked softly.
'Did you want me to kiss you?'

'No!' Theresa said abruptly. 'I'm tired. I want to
fix a place to sleep.' She felt a desperate need to wall
off a little space for her bed, where she could be alone
for a while. 'Maybe if we pull those four fig trees into
a row across that corner, and that Norfolk pine,' she
suggested, pointing to them.

'All right,' Luke said. 'We will fix you your own
little Garden of Eden. Let's put this miniature lemon
tree in there, too. It adds the right atmosphere. Too
bad it isn't an apple tree.' He chuckled as he tugged

the heavy plant on its castored stand into place. 'Do you suppose things would have turned out differently if Adam had sucked on a lemon?'

'I doubt it,' Theresa said drily. 'Eve would probably have just added a little extra sugar.'

'So you think the attraction between the sexes was inevitable?' Luke asked, pushing a fig tree into the line-up.

'I'm afraid so,' Theresa replied, wondering what Luke was leading up to now. She did not feel like engaging in a debate with Luke about sexual attraction at the moment. She did not want to think about sexual attraction. She wanted to be alone so that she could stop fighting sexual attraction for a while. 'There,' she said, opening her bed and changing the subject. 'All I need now is some sheets and a pillow. It's too warm for a blanket.'

'Mmm-hmm,' Luke said. 'I know where they are. I found them today when I was looking for a place to stash those erotic pictures. I pity poor Harry if he needs that kind of stuff to get him aroused. I certainly don't, not with you around. They really opened a can of worms, didn't they, Adam and Eve? There I'll be, sleeping on a bed that's big enough for three or four people, simply because if you and I were there together we wouldn't be able to leave each other alone. Strange, isn't it?'

'Speak for yourself,' Theresa snapped, her nerves having wound themselves even tighter at Luke's statement that, with her around, he needed no pictures to arouse him.

'Tch, tch, such a short memory,' Luke chided. 'Sometimes I wonder...'

'All right! So it works both ways. The fact is, I'm sleeping here, and you're sleeping there! Now will you just drop the subject and get me some sheets?' Theresa asked plaintively.

'In a minute,' Luke said. He folded his arms across his chest and cocked his head, looking thoughtful. 'Tell me, Terry, love, is the only reason I want you here some primitive, elemental urge that says the big, strong caveman must demonstrate his courage to the woman? Is the reason you're here because nature says you're supposed to find the biggest, strongest caveman around to be your mate? Or is there more than that between us?'

Theresa glared and advanced toward Luke. 'Right now, caveman,' she said, 'the only thing between you and another trip into the wild blue yonder is the fact that I'm too tired, and the only reason I'm here is insanity. Will you get me those sheets or do I have to...'

'Shhh,' Luke said, raising his head and listening intently. 'I thought I heard something.'

'What?' Theresa whispered. She could hear no unusual sound. Then suddenly, from the kitchen, came a loud crash and the sound of glass breaking.

CHAPTER FIVE

THERESA let out a gasp and instinctively flung herself into the protecting circle of Luke's arms. Almost immediately she realised what she had done and stiffened, trying to pull herself free. When Luke only tightened his grip, she looked up at him and frowned. Instead of looking frightened, he was smiling broadly.

'Caveman save you,' he whispered. 'I think it might only be from the cat, though, knocking over a jar. Shall we go and see?'

Theresa nodded, and together they tiptoed along a wall until they reached the kitchen door. All was quiet.

'Shall I turn on the light?' Luke whispered in Theresa's ear.

She nodded, ready to spring into action, while Luke reached his hand inside and found the light switch. The fluorescent bulbs flooded the room with light. There was still no more noise.

Luke motioned toward the kitchen, his eyebrows raised questioningly.

'Very slowly,' Theresa mouthed, nodding.

They inched into the room. There was no one else there. Nor had the source of the noise been the cat, who was sleeping in his basket by the refrigerator.

'What in the devil...look over there, Theresa,' Luke said. He pointed to the small breakfast-table. On it was lying a large grapefruit. One pane of the old, multi-paned window behind the table was broken.

'Someone must have been playing toss the grapefruit and missed,' Luke said, starting for the object.

'Stop! Don't go near that!' Theresa cried.

Luke stopped, frowning. 'You don't think it's some sort of bomb, do you?' he said incredulously. 'It looks like a perfectly ordinary grapefruit.'

'Maybe it is, but... Oh, lord!' She leaped across the room and flipped off the lights. 'Let's get out of here,' she said, grabbing Luke's arm and pulling him along with her. 'Someone could have done that so you'd investigate,' she explained when they were back in the living-room, 'and there you would have been, in front of the windows, a perfect target with the lights on.'

'Phew.' Luke looked shaken. He looked toward the french doors at the front of the living-room. 'The lights are on in here, too,' he said.

'Yes, but it's less likely someone would stand right out in front and take a shot. There are streetlights out there, all of those plants in the way, and they might have to stand and wait quite a while unless they got you to the window with another grapefruit,' Theresa said. 'What's out back? An alley?'

'A walled yard with a gate in it,' Luke replied. 'A dark walled yard. Maybe what I heard first was the click of the gate.' He frowned. 'What if that grapefruit goes boom?'

'I don't think it will,' Theresa replied. 'If it was anything sinister, I think it was just to attract your attention. I don't think the Brimstones are up to building a fancy bomb. It might just have been vandals, though. They throw rocks through windows all the time in Chicago. Maybe here they throw grapefruit.'

Luke began pacing back and forth among the plants, his movements agitated. Now and then he glanced towards the french doors. At last he went to one, peered out carefully, and then inspected the latch.

'Not much security there,' he said, rattling the door. He returned to Theresa and stood in front of her, his expression tense and serious. 'I don't know whether it's vandals or real criminals out there, but I don't like the idea of you sleeping in here,' he said. 'It would be damned easy for someone to get in and grab you. You take the bedroom. Old Harry has shutters on those windows. No person or grapefruit can get in.'

'Luke,' Theresa said soothingly, trying to calm him, 'no one's likely to come in and try to grab me. Why would they want to? Besides, in case you've forgotten, I'm very dangerous to grab.'

'Not if someone has a gun,' Luke replied. 'Don't argue.'

'Oh, for heaven's sake,' Theresa grumbled. She did not want to sleep in that weird bedroom. Even without the pictures, it brought to mind only one word. Sex. She went to the french doors and inspected them. 'These really are bad,' she said, frowning. Anyone with minimal skills at breaking in would have no trouble. 'We'll have to do something about them tomorrow.'

'Then do as I say,' Luke said firmly. 'Go in the bedroom and lock the door.'

'I will not! If it's not safe for me out here, it's even less safe for you. You don't know karate.'

Luke's eyes narrowed dangerously. 'Then,' he growled, 'I have the perfect solution.' With a quick move, he picked Theresa up, tossed her over his shoulder, and marched into the bedroom. 'There,' he said, putting her down and locking the door behind him. He turned and faced Theresa, who was standing, glowering at him. 'Now we're both safe.'

'I don't care much for your caveman act,' she said coldly, 'and I don't feel particularly safe in here with you. Open that door and let me out of here. I do not want to sleep in this . . . this disgusting room.' Nor did she especially want to give Luke another demonstration of her karate skills. But if he was going to be so unreasonable . . .

'I don't give a damn whether you do or not!' Luke roared, the usual velvet of his voice shredded to harsh tatters. 'This is not the time for a petty argument about the décor, when your life might be at stake. You know damn well you're safe with me. Can you guarantee there's not some maniac running loose out there?' He grabbed Theresa's wrist as she started to raise her hand to gesture. 'And don't try any of your fancy moves on me, either,' he snarled, 'because I'll just keep getting up and coming after you until I win, unless you kill me first.'

Theresa stared at him in disbelief. This was certainly a very different Luke Thorndike. 'But, Luke,' she said softly, trying a new tactic since he obviously meant what he said, 'my suitcase is in the other room. I need to get my pyjamas and my toothbrush.'

'Not a chance,' Luke replied. 'You're staying right here. You can wear my pyjama top, and Harry, hospitable soul that he is, has a huge supply of new toothbrushes, fancy soaps, and all that.'

Theresa cast a sidelong glance at the huge, round bed beneath its shimmering, satin cover. 'I suppose I could sleep in the bathtub,' she said.

'You do, and I'll turn on the water,' Luke threatened. He rubbed his forehead. 'For God's sake, be reasonable, Theresa. If it will make you feel better, we can pile those fur pillows down the middle of the bed. But believe me, right now I'm not in the mood for any hanky-panky, and I assume you aren't, either. Or did you become a detective because the excitement turns you on?'

'Certainly not!' Theresa denied hotly. She eyed the bed again. If the word 'sin' were embroidered in the bedspread, she thought, it could not look more suggestively lush. 'If the sheets are satin, I *am* sleeping in the bathtub,' she said defiantly. She walked stiffly over to the bed, threw the pillows to the floor, and pulled off the cover, revealing sheets that were not satin, but were white with little red hearts all over them. The bed wiggled strangely as Theresa felt it. 'Good lord, it's a water-bed. I'll get seasick.'

'No, you won't,' Luke said. 'They're very comfortable.' He knelt and arranged the pillows in a row down the centre of the bed, his jaw jutting at an uncompromising angle.

Theresa watched, her hands clenched at her sides, wondering irrelevantly whether she was dreaming or she was actually going to sleep in that bed with Luke. Nothing for the last half-hour or so seemed quite real, starting with the grapefruit coming through the window. She felt like laughing hysterically at the sight of the bed wobbling in waves beneath Luke's weight as he got up from it and stood up. It was going to be like that night on the sail-boat, going up and down, up and down. She clapped her hand over her mouth and followed Luke with her eyes as, still frowning, he went to the ornate, lacquered dresser, opened a drawer, and pulled out a set of pyjamas.

'Here,' he said, thrusting the pyjama top towards her.

Theresa took it and stared at it. It was light blue silk, with LT embroidered on the pocket. Somehow, she hadn't thought Luke would go for initials on his clothing. 'LT,' she said thoughtfully.

'Theresa,' Luke said, his voice grating impatiently, 'would you please get your act together and go and put that on? The toothbrushes are in the drawer to the right, below the lavatory. If you want to take a shower, the knob in the middle is the one to turn.'

'You needn't treat me like an idiot,' Theresa said crossly.

'Then don't act like one,' Luke countered. 'Get moving. Or are you nailed to that spot?'

Theresa glared at him. 'Don't be so bossy,' she said. She turned and marched into the bathroom, locking the door behind her. For a moment, the brightness of the crystal chandelier reflecting from the mirrored walls dazzled her eyes. There was scarcely an inch that wasn't mirrored, and she had the uncomfortable feeling that there were several people in the room with her. Maybe a hot shower would steam the mirrors over. She turned it on, then got in and stood still beneath the pulsing spray. 'I'm not going to hurry,' she muttered. There was no reason to hurry. She wasn't going to be able to sleep, anyhow, with Luke on the other side of that flimsy barricade.

But that's silly, she told herself as she dried herself with a huge pink towel. You can trust Luke. He said you could. He didn't bother you last night, did he? She put on the pyjama top, which came to several inches above her knees, and rolled up the cuffs. Last night, she knew, had been different. The setting had been different, she had been different. She hadn't re-evaluated how she felt about him then. She had only wanted to protect him. Or had she? She was no longer sure. Luke was different tonight, too. Masterful. Protective. If someone had asked, she would have said she'd hate a man to treat her that way, as if she were helpless and fragile, but to be totally honest she hadn't minded that much. She frowned at her reflection as she brushed her teeth. Was she, after all, just a cave-woman looking for her strong protective hero, and not the tough, independent woman she had imagined? Or was it that adding that quality to all of Luke's other unique qualities made an almost irresistible combination?

'Theresa Long,' she said, bending forward and addressing her reflection seriously, 'just who is it that you don't trust?'

There was an impatient rap on the door. 'Are you going to stay in there all night talking to yourself?' Luke demanded.

'No, sir,' Theresa said meekly, opening the door. 'It's all yours.' She could feel his eyes following her as she walked across the toe-tickling fur rug to the bed and bent to turn the sheet back. Just as she lay down, she heard the door click shut behind him. The bed writhed beneath her as if it were alive. An experimental kick with one leg produced another orgy of activity, and Theresa smiled to herself. It was rather fun. She caught sight of her reflection in the mirrored ceiling, and spent several minutes bouncing the bed and watching herself apparently bobbing on a sea of red hearts. This wasn't so bad, after all. She had been silly to worry and make a fuss. No wonder Luke was disgusted with her. She would apologise to him—in the morning. Better to keep him cross for now. She heard the bathroom door open, and quickly turned over and pretended to be asleep.

Luke turned off the light, then sat down heavily on the bed, sending it into a convulsion of activity. Theresa giggled in spite of herself.

'What's so funny?' Luke asked.

'I feel as if I ought to sing "Row, Row, Row Your Boat",' Theresa replied. 'Did you ever sing that, you know, like a round? A round in a round bed.' She giggled again. '"Row, row, row your boat,"' she began, 'come on, Luke, join in, "gently down the stream, merrily, merrily, merrily, merrily, life is but a dream. Row, row, row..."'

'Theresa,' Luke growled, 'be quiet and go to sleep. I am not in the mood for singing.'

'Grouch,' Theresa muttered. 'Go to sleep yourself. Maybe you'll be in a better mood in the morning.'

'That,' Luke said, 'is exactly what I plan to do.'

Theresa closed her eyes. She was obviously going to be very safe with Luke tonight. Too bad she didn't feel especially happy about it. Oh, well, there was always tomorrow. She ought to be able to find some excuse to be here again, with Luke. Her eyes flew open. What was she thinking? She could almost hear her mother saying, 'Shame on you, Theresa!' That thought made her giggle again.

Luke turned, starting the bed tossing and waving again.

'Theresa,' he demanded, 'what is wrong with you?'

'Nothing.' She tried not to giggle, but couldn't help it. 'I think this water-bed tickles my funny bone,' she gasped out between chuckles.

Luke groaned. 'As long as you're awake, would you mind rubbing my neck? It's aching like the devil. I think that fall gave me whiplash.'

'Oh, no! I knew you should have gone to the hospital,' Theresa said, dismayed out of her fit of giggles. She moved next to the fur pillows and reached for Luke's neck, then threw the top pillow out of the way. 'There,' she said, beginning to knead Luke's neck and shoulders. 'Tell me where it helps the most. I'm so sorry I hurt you. That was about the dumbest trick I've ever pulled.'

'Mmm,' Luke said, sighing in relief. 'Yeah. Right there. Beats me how someone as small as you are could do that. Your hands are strong, too.'

'You should see me break a board,' Theresa said, kneading her way out to Luke's shoulders and back. His skin felt so smooth and warm, but beneath it his muscles were tightly knotted. She got to her knees so that she could apply more pressure, flinging more pillows out of the way. 'How does that feel?' she asked, experimentally pounding up and down his back with the side of her hand.

'Heavenly,' Luke replied. He lifted his head. 'You aren't getting ready to break my back, are you?'

'No, silly, just relax. Shut your eyes. And mouth. You're tied up in knots.'

'Yes'm,' Luke said, lowering his head again.

As Theresa kneaded and massaged, she could feel Luke gradually relax, the tense muscles becoming supple beneath her hands. His breathing became soft and regular. He was asleep. She smiled wryly to herself. Poor darling. He must have been in quite a lot of pain. It was so nice to be able to make him feel better, since it was her fault in the first place. Slowly she lightened her touch, until she stopped, kneeling beside him, looking wistfully at his broad back, his dark head against the ridiculous, heart-covered pillow. She wished she could lie down next to him, her cheek against his shoulder, instead of retreating across the bed to her side...no, that would be asking for trouble. The pillows were gone now, and she didn't want to disturb him by putting them back. They could easily find themselves in each other's arms, and that might lead to more serious consequences. She knew Luke wanted her, she knew he cared enough to carry her in here to keep her safe. But, before she made love to him, she needed to know that he loved her and wanted to keep her with him forever. Most of all, she needed to know that, if he made such a promise, she could trust him to keep it. To have him for only a short time and then lose him again would break her heart.

Carefully, so as to keep the shuddering bed from awakening him, Theresa lowered herself and moved a short distance away.

'Goodnight, Luke,' she whispered softly. To her surprise, he answered, apparently only half asleep.

'G'night,' he mumbled. He turned and threw one long arm across Theresa. 'C'mere, love,' he said, pulling her toward him. 'Turn a little. Put your back against me. That's right.' He tightened his grip, tucking her into the curve of his body, his arm snuggled beneath her breasts. A soft sound of contentment came from his throat, and then he was fast asleep, his chest rising and falling against Theresa's back.

At Luke's touch, Theresa had tensed, wanting to be close and yet still afraid to. But, as the minutes passed, she, too, became drowsily content. If this was trouble, she was all for it, she thought with a rueful smile. Whether there was some vandal out there with a mania for throwing grapefruit instead of rocks, or someone more sinister, she didn't know, but whoever it was she would like to thank him. She closed her eyes and drifted off to sleep, still smiling.

Theresa awoke with a start to the sound of a car door slamming and Luke's voice calling out, 'Thanks!' Good heavens, where had he been and what time was it?

She jumped out of bed and ran to peep out of the french doors. A bright red foreign sports car was parked at the kerb. Luke was coming up the front path, followed by an attractive redhead wearing tight jeans and a T-shirt that clung to her ample bosom like wallpaper. Both were carrying grocery bags. Well! Never let it be said that Luke Thorndike didn't work fast, Theresa thought grimly. He probably knew that in that horizontal-striped shirt that made his broad shoulders look even broader, and those tight jeans, almost any woman would drop everything and follow him. It looked as if that one was going to follow him right into the house! Oh, no! Theresa looked down at her own scantily clad form. She had better... Before she could gather her wits and beat a swift retreat to the bedroom, the door opened. She froze, hoping the fig tree beside her would hide her, but Luke spotted her immediately.

'Well, hello, sleepyhead,' he said, as unconcerned as if she were fully dressed. 'Did you just get up? This is our neighbour, Patsy Muffett. She wants to see our grapefruit.'

Theresa moved out from behind the fig tree and gave Luke a deadly glance and the woman a frozen smile. 'Nice to meet you,' she said.

'Hi!' said Patsy, a knowing smile on her face as she appraised Theresa's attire. 'Sorry to barge in, but I did want to see that grapefruit. I think I may know where it came from.'

'Come on,' Luke said, leading the way toward the kitchen. 'It's still on the table. I haven't touched the thing yet. I thought maybe one of my enemies had tossed me a yellow grenade.'

'Oh, Luke,' Patsy burbled, 'You're so funny.' She turned to Theresa, who had followed, unable to make up her mind whether she would look any more foolish if she ran off to get dressed or stayed the way she was, in Luke's pyjama top. 'Is Luke always so funny?' she asked.

'A laugh a minute,' Theresa replied drily. 'Where do you think the grapefruit came from?'

'Well, there's this bunch of crazies...' Patsy put down her bag of groceries on the counter and went to pick up the grapefruit. 'It's them, all right,' she said, turning the grapefruit over in her hand. 'See?' On the under side of the grapefruit was written, in black indelible pen, 'Repent. The End Is Near!'

Luke stared at the message, then burst out laughing. 'You mean there's some group that goes around throwing those things through windows?'

Patsy nodded. 'They call themselves Elijah's Prophets. Once in a while one of them gets caught, but most of the time people just clean up the mess and forget it. I can tell you who to call to fix that glass. They had to do mine last winter. Here, I'll write it down for you,' as Luke took out his notepad. She wrote down the name of a glass company, then handed the notepad back. 'It's a shame that had to happen your first night here,' she said, in her gurgly Southern drawl, 'before you had a chance to find out about all the silly things that go on here in the Quarter. I declare, sometimes it's like living in a zoo.' She smiled at Theresa and beamed at Luke. 'I'm so glad I got to meet you. I can see you all have unfinished business, so I'll just run on home now, but if you need anything, just holler. Y'all hear?'

'Yes, ma'am,' Luke replied, treating her to one of his warmest smiles. 'And thanks again for taking me to the store. We might have starved without you.'

'It was my pleasure,' Patsy said. 'Bye, now.'

Theresa watched as she bounced off, with Luke, ever the gentleman, escorting her to the door. He returned and lifted one eyebrow at Theresa, who was still standing by the table, trying to decide whether to say anything first, or give in to an impulse to start throwing things at him without warning. His mouth quirked into a mischievous smile.

'I'll bet you're thinking the same thing I am,' he said. 'We ought to send Elijah's Prophets a donation.'

'That is *not* what I was thinking!' Theresa said loudly. 'Couldn't you have been a little more obvious? "Look, there's Theresa in my pyjama top. She just got up." I have never been so embarrassed in my life! Your bosomy friend certainly thought she had everything figured out. "Unfinished business"!'

Luke rubbed his chin. 'Well, I suppose I could have said, see that person in the blue pyjama top over there behind the fig tree? That's Theresa. She stands there like that, by the window, night and day. I doubt Patsy would have bought that, though. Or is her bosom what's bothering you?'

'Certainly not! The least you could have done was wake me before you left to go... wherever you went.'

'No, I couldn't,' Luke said, shaking his head and smiling ruefully. 'As soon as I woke up and looked at you there beside me, I knew I had to get up and out of there in a hurry. There was only one thing on my mind. So I sneaked out and let you sleep, planning to walk to some nearby store and find something for our breakfast. Little Miss Muffett was out in front watering her tuffets, and she offered to take me in her car to a real supermarket to shop. I thought surely you'd be up and dressed by the time I got back.' His smile widened slowly, his eyes sweeping down Theresa's form and back to her eyes. 'Or were you just waiting around in that outfit to tempt me again?'

'No!' Theresa snapped, cursing the warmth that spread through her and set her cheeks aflame. That smile of his made her only too aware of what was still occupying his mind, and it was very difficult to remember why she had been so upset with him. His explanation had sounded completely reasonable, and if he didn't stop smiling at her like that ... She gave herself a mental shake. 'I'll get dressed right away and help with breakfast,' she said, starting to hurry past him. He reached out and caught her.

'Wait a minute,' he said, pulling her to him and then locking his hands behind her. 'You haven't even asked if I saw the Brimstones while I was out.'

'Well ... well, did you?' Theresa asked, looking up at him, but scarcely able to breathe. It seemed as if Luke's hands, firm against her back, were burning through the silk of his pyjama top and setting her skin on fire.

'No,' Luke replied, 'but I could have. They could have been parked in that black car across the street. Patsy could have been an accomplice, hired to bring me to them.' He put his fingers beneath Theresa's chin and caressed back and forth, his eyes sparkling with a gentle mirth. 'It's a good thing I'm only keeping you around for company, isn't it? Between embarrassment and jealousy, and wanting the same thing I want, you don't keep your mind on detective work very well.'

Theresa swallowed hard, feeling tears welling up. It was true. She had been so caught up in her own feelings that she hadn't thought once about the Brimstones. 'I'm sorry,' she said in a small voice. 'I know I'm not being much help. I was certainly wrong about that ridiculous grapefruit.'

'Ah, yes, the grapefruit.' Luke lifted Theresa's chin. 'Look me in the eyes, Theresa,' he said. 'Can you honestly say that there wasn't some point last night when you were very glad it came crashing in through the window?'

'Well, I . . . n-no,' Theresa replied, unable to avoid Luke's eyes and knowing that it would be useless to deny it, when that was exactly what she had thought. What, she wondered with a shiver, would Luke think if he knew she'd even thought of inventing some excuse for tonight?

'And are you still glad?' Luke persisted.

Theresa frowned. What was he driving at now? 'Why shouldn't I be?' she asked.

'Answer me first,' Luke said firmly.

'Yes, I'm still glad,' Theresa replied. Going to sleep in Luke's arms had been heavenly. Just remembering it was dangerous to her equilibrium. What was the point in lying about it when she felt herself melting closer and closer against him, her eyes more and more fascinated with the soft curves of his mouth?

'Good,' Luke said. 'I think we're making progress.'

'I still don't understand,' Theresa complained. 'I haven't had any coffee yet, and my mind isn't working very well.' Not to mention the fact that she was so aware of every inch of Luke's body against hers that she could scarcely think at all.

'Well,' Luke said, smiling now and beginning to stroke her back with devastating effect, 'I was afraid you might focus on the fact that if the grapefruit hadn't frightened us, you'd have slept on your bed, I'd have awakened you when I got up, and we'd have gone off in search of breakfast together, thus avoiding your unpleasant encounter with our neighbour, and eliminating my need to get so well acquainted with her.'

'Oh,' Theresa said. It was all so complicated. 'I didn't think about that angle at all,' she admitted with a sigh. 'Why did you think that I would?'

'Because you've been so afraid to get close to me,' Luke answered, 'and even more afraid to admit that you wanted to.' He squeezed her shoulders. 'Now, run along and get dressed. I'm not going to kiss you now, because in that outfit, the temptation might be too much for both of us, and I don't think we're ready to get that close yet.' He ran his hands down Theresa's body and then patted her bottom. 'Scoot,' he said.

Theresa walked slowly into the bedroom, rather than scooting, feeling as if she were sleepwalking. Somewhere along the line, she seemed to have lost control of the situation, she mused. She had been going to keep herself and Luke under control, and now he was the one who had the upper hand. She had better find some way to at least get control of herself, or she was going to find herself making love to Luke on his terms, and not complaining a bit!

CHAPTER SIX

'How does French toast made with thick slices of French bread sound?' Luke asked when Theresa returned to the kitchen, dressed in navy blue slacks and a white cotton cable sweater.

'Fattening,' Theresa replied. 'Only one slice for me.'

'Now, Terry, love——' Luke began, but she interrupted him.

'Don't "Terry, love" me,' she said. 'I know how much I should eat, and I'm not going to let you fatten me up for slaughter.'

She had decided while she dressed that she was going to have to regain the upper hand in everything and not let Luke cajole and badger her into doing things. No matter how far their relationship did or didn't go, it was a bad precedent to set. She hadn't worked so hard to become an independent woman these last few years, just to let him turn her into a submissive little mouse again. If she had been more assertive five years ago, she might not have fallen so completely under his spell, and felt so devastated when she discovered that, like her father, his feet were made of clay.

Luke shrugged. 'I certainly wouldn't want you to outgrow those trousers. You fill them out rather nicely now. Nice outfit.'

'Quent likes me to dress well when I'm representing the agency,' Theresa replied, relieved that he didn't argue about the French toast, and trying to ignore the warm glow that followed his compliment. 'Which reminds me, I'd better start hunting for Toby McDonald as soon as we're through breakfast. It's almost noon now, and since it's Saturday, everything should be in full swing before long. What can I do to help?'

'Just pour the coffee,' Luke replied. 'Everything else is ready.' He carried their plates to the table. 'Tell me about this McDonald chap,' he suggested as he began to attack his breakfast with gusto.

He would be one of those people who can eat everything and never gain weight, Theresa thought bitterly, watching him. She frowned, then answered, 'He's a fifty-one-year-old building contractor. He came down here a couple of years ago for a jazz festival and met Carmelita, the dancer. When he didn't come home when he was supposed to, his wife came and found him and dragged him back home. He was very apologetic and said it would never happen again. His wife told him if it did, he needn't come back. Well, it seems to have happened again. He packed everything, including his most treasured possession, an old trumpet that used to belong to Louis Armstrong, into his car and left. We think he's in New Orleans from some credit card purchases he made. Anyway, now his wife's changed her mind. She wants him back, but she's afraid to come after him herself and tell him. I'm supposed to find him and convey the message and a letter from Mrs McDonald. After that, it's up to fate, I guess.'

'So,' Luke said, smiling broadly, 'today we interview dancers.'

Theresa looked down at her plate and then directly back at Luke. 'No,' she said, 'today *I* interview dancers. It's my job, and I think I'd better do it myself. I'm sure you could use some time alone to get started on your writing.'

Luke leaned back in his chair and scowled. 'As I recall,' he said, his voice rough around the edges, 'you told me you wanted me to help you because I might be able to find out more than you could from the ladies. I can't think of any reason why that wouldn't still be true. Have you some lame-brained idea that keeping me out of those dens of moderate iniquity is going to improve my moral fibre? Because if you do, believe me, Theresa, I've seen things a lot more sinful before and probably will again.'

'I am not the least bit concerned with your moral fibre,' Theresa denied hotly. 'The point is simply that I want to do the job myself. I'm not worried about my moral fibre, and I certainly am not worried about yours.'

'Well, maybe I'm worried about you going into those places alone,' Luke said, still frowning. 'In fact, I don't want you to do it. Someone might mistake you for one of the dancers in street clothes and make a grab for you.'

'He'll be sorry if he does,' Theresa replied. 'You seem to forget about that. Or doesn't it fit your image of me as a poor little helpless female? Just because I let you get away with playing caveman last night it doesn't mean anyone else can. Or that you're going to again, either,' she added, as Luke shot her a sharp glance.

Luke rubbed his forehead and sighed. 'I guess I should have kissed you, after all,' he said.

'And just what does that mean?' Theresa snapped. 'Do you think that if you keep me sexually aroused you'll be able to dictate what I'm to do or not to do? If that's what you think, I've got news for you, Luke Thorndike. I may have a weak moment now and then, but generally I don't like being bullied and bossed around.'

'I *should* have kissed you,' Luke said positively. His mouth curved into a slow smile. 'I probably should have done more than that. You're even more frustrated than I am.'

'You're crazy!' Theresa said, taking a last swallow of her coffee. She stood up. 'Not only that,' she said, 'but you are so egotistical that you turn me off completely. How you can twist around the fact that I want to go out and do the job that I came to do by myself into some wild idea that that means I'm a mass of sexual frustrations that only you can relieve, I can't imagine.'

'Very simple,' Luke replied, his eyes bright with mischievous lights. 'Before you got dressed, you were all cuddly and warm and lovable. You would have been happy to have me come with you anywhere, I'll wager. Now you're a regular shrew. Tell me, Kate, what will it take to tame you? Several more nights on that bed? I think that's what tamed the original Kate, not the bard's immortal words.'

'You would!' Theresa glared at him. 'Unfortunately, I have no desire to be tamed by you or anyone else. You can take me the way I am or leave me alone, I don't care. I'm going right now. You stay here. You should be quite safe from the Brimstones here in the daytime, but for heaven's sake, don't open the door without looking first. I'll be back by five.'

Luke stood and followed Theresa to the door, looking thoughtful. 'All right, I'll stay here this time,' he said. 'Maybe you need to try it alone to be convinced that it might go better with my help, and that it doesn't take anything away from you to have me along. Be careful. I'm going to be worried about you.'

'You don't need to be,' Theresa said tightly. 'I don't spend all of my time in Chicago in the best neighbourhoods.'

'I know,' Luke replied. 'That worries me, too.' He bent suddenly and kissed Theresa's cheek. 'By the way,' he said, as she looked at him, startled, 'I have a question for you.' He drew an imaginary line down the centre of Theresa's body with his finger. 'If you were painted red on this side...' he pointed to her right, 'and green on this side...' he pointed to her left, 'would you be two different people, or still one person?'

'That's a silly question. One person, of course,' Theresa replied.

'Yes,' Luke said, 'but if one person saw only the red side, and another person saw only the green, they might think you were two different people, mightn't they?'

'I suppose so.' Theresa frowned. 'What is this green and red person nonsense all about?'

Luke grinned. 'A little something for you to think about while you're out pounding the pavement. Keeps you from getting bored. Just don't get to thinking too hard about it and forget what you're doing. And don't forget to keep an eye out for the Brimstones. They might come up with the idea of taking you hostage to get to me, since they've seen us together a couple of times now.'

'I'll be careful, Luke,' Theresa said impatiently. 'Stop playing mother hen. I don't like it any better than you do.' Which was, she decided, as she headed for Bourbon Street, not quite the truth. There was something very comforting about having him fuss over her. Why should that be, when having Quentin do the same thing, as he often did, simply annoyed her? And what did Luke mean by that strange question about green and red people? If she knew him at all, it had nothing to do with green and red, but meant something much more complicated.

Theresa joined the milling throng on the part of Bourbon Street that was permanently closed to traffic. There were, she knew, several places that advertised shows featuring exotic dancers. She might as well start enquiring about Carmelita at the first one she came to.

It was between shows in the first place she entered. Scantily clad waitresses were bringing drinks to the patrons, who were seated at tiny tables in the smoky, dimly lit room.

'I don't want a ticket,' Theresa said to the leering man who barred her way. 'A friend of mine told me to look up a dancer he used to know named Carmelita when I was in town, but he wasn't sure where she worked. Do you know her?'

'You a dancer?' the man asked, looking Theresa up and down appraisingly.

'No.' Theresa grimaced. 'I used to dance some, but I had to quit. Back trouble. I work in a department store in Chicago now.'

The man looked more pleasant, almost sympathetic, Theresa thought. She had chosen the right approach. He nodded. 'Them bumps and grinds can do that to you,' he said. 'We don't have any Carmelita here, but you can go on back and see if any of the girls know where you can find her.' He pointed. 'Past the stage and through that door.'

'Thanks,' said Theresa, beaming. 'Thanks a lot.' She made her way backstage, where a dozen or so girls were repairing make-up, changing costumes, or simply sitting and staring into space. A tall brunette looked at Theresa curiously.

'You aren't the new girl, are you?' she asked, her expression clearly incredulous.

Theresa was momentarily taken aback, then she grinned. 'I'm afraid not. Wish I was good enough. Or tall enough.' She repeated her story about her search for Carmelita.

'Don't know her,' said the tall brunette. She turned her head and raised her voice. 'Anyone here know where to find a Carmelita? This gal's lookin' for her.'

Most of the girls shook their heads, but a black-haired beauty came forward.

'Whatcha want to find Carmelita for?' she asked, looking suspiciously at Theresa.

'I met a fellow in Chicago who used to know her,' Theresa explained, not surprised at the question. She expected the dancers to be protective of each other. 'He wanted me to look her up and tell her hello for him. I think he's still carrying a torch for her.'

'Lots of guys do that,' said the dancer. She shrugged. 'I think she's still working at the Moonbeam Club. It's across the street and down a block. You can't miss it.'

Theresa thanked the girl and went back out to the street, blinking in the bright sunlight. If Carmelita was still at the Moonbeam Club, this was going to be easier than she'd thought. Wouldn't Luke be surprised that she'd done so well without him? Thinking of Luke reminded her of the Brimstone brothers, and she quickly scanned the crowd. They were not in the area that she could see, but she decided to zigzag back and forth on her way down the street and keep her eyes open for the pair. Too bad they weren't painted red and green, she thought wryly. They would be a lot easier to spot.

She repeated her story at the Moonbeam Club which was, she discovered, not much different from the previous place, except that the show was in full swing, and the patrons were making encouraging comments on the dancers' efforts. The response to her question, however, was different and discouraging.

'She ain't here no more,' the man said. 'She quit last week and went off with some guy.'

'Some guy?' Theresa asked, her heart sinking. Had Toby McDonald really gone all the way this time?

'Yeah. A sailor. I think she's living with him someplace, but I don't know where.'

Theresa breathed a sigh of relief. It wasn't Toby. 'Do you think one of the girls might know?' she asked.

'Could be,' the man replied. 'If you wanta wait until after the show, you can ask them.'

Theresa waited and asked, but the girls were unable, or unwilling, to tell her. 'Did she ever mention a Toby McDonald?' she asked, thinking it sadly unlikely that a young woman in love with a sailor would have had any cause to do so. To her surprise, several of the girls laughed at her question.

'You mean that short, bald guy from Chicago?' one of them asked. 'He used to hang around here all the time, a couple of years back. Nearly drove Carmelita crazy. Harry Jefferson finally ran him off. She was going with Harry, then. Harry's kind of a famous artist.'

'I know,' Theresa said. If that wasn't a strange co-incidence! Luke's friend Harry had been involved with Carmelita, too. 'Well, thanks anyway,' she said. Discouraged, she wandered farther down Bourbon Street, then turned off on to a side street and found a pavement café where she sat down and ordered a Coke. Without the Carmelita lead, she had no idea where to look for the errant Mr McDonald. He might not be in New Orleans at all. Or he might have become infatuated with another dancer. She should have thought of that before. Now, it was going to be hard to go back and ask a different question. She might need Luke's help, after all. After the way she'd acted this morning, he might not want to help her. He was such a strange man. So funny, and yet so serious. Red and green. Two people in one.

'That's what he meant!' Theresa said aloud, then looked around, embarrassed. She smiled to herself. No one had noticed her revelation. Two people in one. Was he trying to tell her that she could be both a competent, self-reliant private investigator, and a woman

who was . . . what had he said . . . warm, and cuddly
and lovable at the same time? She wasn't sure that
was possible. She didn't feel as if she could. When
one side appeared, the other seemed to vanish. Maybe
Luke only thought she could because he was so good
at changing back and forth, chameleon-like. Maybe
he only wanted her to because he had the upper hand
when she was under his spell. She sighed. If she dis-
agreed with him, that was certain to start an argument.

She finished her drink and then looked at her watch.
Almost four o'clock. She hated to go back and tell
Luke of her failure, but she might as well get it over
with. Maybe he'd have some helpful ideas.

Theresa decided not to plough through the crowds
on Bourbon Street again, instead going to Dauphine
before heading back toward Luke's apartment. There
were still plenty of people to dodge, but she had not
gone far before she spotted the Brimstone brothers
walking along briskly in the same direction as she was
going. I wonder where they're going, she thought,
quickening her pace to keep up with them, but staying
far enough back to be able to duck out of sight if
necessary. When they reached Dumaine, they turned
toward Luke's apartment, but stayed on the opposite
side of the street from it. Theresa's pulse accelerated.
She crossed Dauphine, then peered carefully around
the corner. The Brimstones were walking very slowly
now, staying in the shadows cast by the late afternoon
sun. From time to time they would look over at Luke's
apartment, then put their heads together in serious
conversation. Theresa slipped around the corner and
got as close as she dared without attracting their attention, ready to vanish into a nearby doorway if

necessary. The men came to a stop across from Luke's apartment. They looked back and forth again. One of them nodded and looked at his watch. Then they turned and came in Theresa's direction. She flattened herself against the wall and held her breath, hoping they would not look, then breathed a sigh of relief after they had passed. As soon as she dared, she peeked out, saw them round the corner on to Dauphine again, and then flew across the street and let herself into the apartment.

'Luke!' she called. She peered into the bedroom, then hurried towards the kitchen. 'Luke! Where are...' She stopped. Well! When the cat's away, she thought. Luke and Patsy were sitting at the table, a bowl of shrimps between them.

'Patsy brought over some of her spiced shrimp,' Luke said, giving Theresa a rather defiant look. 'You ought to try them.'

'Maybe later,' Theresa replied, noticing that Patsy looked very smug.

'I was just trying to talk Luke into going to a place I know that has absolutely the best seafood gumbo,' Patsy said, giving Theresa an overly sweet smile. 'Would you like to come along?'

'No, thanks,' Theresa said, eyeing Luke, who was now looking decidedly uncomfortable. 'I think I'll be staying home this evening. I discovered that some old friends of ours may be dropping in.' She raised her eyebrows meaningfully at Luke. By his startled expression, she could tell that he got her meaning. Now to see if she could get rid of that insidious little shrimp-bearer, so that she could talk to Luke alone. 'Why don't you run along with Patsy?' Theresa asked smoothly, giving him a sugary smile. 'Just be sure you call before you come back. I'd hate for you to be surprised by what you find when you get here.'

The horrified look on Patsy's face was almost too much for Theresa, but she managed to keep a straight face while she waited for Luke to come up with something brilliant to save the situation. He did not disappoint her.

'And miss all the fun?' he said, as if that were out of the question. He shook his head. 'No way. Sorry, Patsy, I'm afraid I'll have to take a raincheck.'

'That's all right. I understand,' she said quickly. 'Old friends, and all that.' She gathered up her shrimps and started toward the door all in one movement. 'I hope you all have a...a real good time,' she said. ''Bye, now.'

As soon as Patsy was out the door, Theresa burst out laughing. 'Nice work,' she said as Luke returned, his own eyes twinkling. 'Sorry the Brimstones spoiled your evening out.'

'Not bad yourself,' he replied. 'And don't go jumping to foolish conclusions. I'm almost glad the boys are coming. I was wondering how to get out of that gumbo feast without being rude to Patsy. She's as persistent as a bad case of poison ivy.' He sat back down at the table and then frowned. 'Damn! She left her car keys,' he said, picking up a pair of keys attached to a small ring.

'I'll put them by the telephone. She'll probably be back for them in a few minutes,' Theresa said. She carried the keys into the living-room, then returned. 'Want to hear all about it?' she asked.

'In a minute,' Luke replied. He turned his chair sideways to the table and patted his knee. 'Come here, Terry, love. We have some unfinished business from this morning.'

'What kind of business?' Theresa asked warily. From the gleam in his eyes, it was apparent that thoughts of the Brimstone brothers were not uppermost in his mind. Was he still brooding about her alter ego? This was hardly the time for that!

'I made a mistake this morning,' Luke said. 'I want to rectify it. Either come here, or...' he gave her a devilish smile, 'I'll come and get you.'

'No!' Theresa backed away, frowning. 'Luke Thorndike, you stop this nonsense,' she said, as he got up and started toward her. 'I thought you understood what I was saying. The Brimstone brothers...' she turned and ran into the living-room, putting a potted palm tree between them, 'are planning something. I followed them all the way down...' she circled the palm, 'Dauphine Street. They came down Dumaine and looked at your apartment, and then...' she jumped away as Luke made a grab for her '...they went back.'

'Casing the joint, huh?' Luke said, moving stealthily towards Theresa, like a prowling cat. 'And then they are going to...' he lunged suddenly and caught Theresa, 'try and catch me napping?'

'It looks as if they're going to,' Theresa snapped, trying to pull herself free. 'Will you pay attention? We need to decide what to do.'

'I've already decided,' Luke said calmly. 'Stop wiggling. I'm going to kiss you.'

'But, Luke,' Theresa pleaded, feeling her heart accelerate in spite of her desire to remain calm and make some sensible plans, 'we can't just pretend nothing's going to happen. You may be in real danger.'

'And so may you,' Luke said softly, caressing Theresa's hair back from her forehead. 'This is the perfect time for a kiss. Think how we'd feel if something terrible did happen, and we'd missed this opportunity.' He smiled slowly. 'Would you want that to happen?'

Theresa felt her knees go weak, just as they had that long-ago day when she had first seen Luke's smile. No, she thought, she would not want that to happen. If he were to be... she dared not finish the thought. She raised her face to his, blinking back the tears that had anticipated her thoughts and filled her eyes. 'No,' she whispered hoarsely. In an instant, Luke's mouth covered hers, so warm and sweet that it took her breath away. She flung her arms around his broad back and clung to him fiercely, responding with abandon to the hunger of his kiss. Her sweet, funny, serious Luke. She adored him so. The wonder of that realisation sent her heart soaring. She murmured soft sounds of happiness, feeling a heightened joy at every sensation of touch and taste that passed between them, as if some barrier had been passed that released her from a prison of restraints. She belonged to Luke Thorndike, for better or worse, whenever and however he might want her.

Luke abandoned her mouth and showered Theresa's face with light little kisses, ending with his lips nuzzling her ear. 'Oh, Terry, love,' he murmured, 'I've waited so long for you to kiss me like that.'

Theresa nuzzled him back, kissing beneath his chin, burying her face against his neck and breathing deeply, absorbing the essence that was uniquely his. 'Maybe the best plan,' she said huskily, 'would be for us to go in the bedroom and lock the door and not come out until the Brimstones have died of old age.' To her surprise, Luke pulled his head back and frowned at her severely.

'Theresa Long,' he scolded, 'are you suggesting what I think you're suggesting? An illicit relationship?'

'Don't tell me the thought hadn't occurred to you,' she said, stiffening and trying to pull herself free of Luke's tight embrace. She felt as if she had suddenly received a splash of cold water in the face. What kind of turnabout was he doing now?

'Of course it had,' he replied, putting his hand behind her neck and pulling it against his chest so that she could feel the vibrations when he chuckled. 'There's nothing wrong with the thought,' he said. 'I'm very flattered. But my job isn't quite finished yet, so I'm afraid you'll have to wait, just as I will. Do you think we can live on kisses until then?'

Theresa groaned. 'I haven't the slightest idea what you're talking about,' she said. 'Between your mysterious job and your red and green people, you have me so confused I hardly know what I think. Do you suppose you could be a little more specific?' She raised her head and looked into Luke's dark eyes, trying to fathom what he was thinking. It was no use, for all he did was smile and shake his head. 'Great,' she grumbled. 'Do you have any magical mumbo jumbo that will make the Brimstones disappear? If not, we'd better try some plain old brain-power to figure out what they might be planning and what we can do to stop them.'

'I like the way you say "we" lately,' Luke said. He brushed Theresa's lips with his own again, then let them linger softly against them.

'Do you suppose,' Theresa said with a sigh, letting her lips move against his, 'that we're just having a dream? I can't think of any other reason we'd be standing here like this, kissing away our future and maybe kissing it goodbye.'

'I think we're beginning to have one,' Luke replied, ending his statement by deepening his kiss again. The telephone rang and he raised his head. 'Damn! Who could that be?'

'Probably just Patsy wanting to know if we found her keys,' Theresa replied. 'You'd better answer. I don't think she's too fond of me.'

Luke answered the telephone, and moments later held it out toward Theresa. 'It's your brother,' he said.

'Maybe he's turned up something on the Brimstones,' Theresa said, taking it. 'Hello, Quent. What's up?' When she hung up a short time later, she shook her head at Luke. 'Nothing definite yet. Quent found out when the Brimstones got out of prison and where they went. It wasn't to Las Vegas. They went to Hollywood. There must be someone there who has it in for you. Quent's going to get in touch with some contacts out there tomorrow.'

'I don't know who it could be,' Luke said, frowning. 'As I said before, success breeds enemies, but I can't imagine anyone that I know hating me enough to want me dead. Well, now that the spell is broken, what shall we do? I'd suggest turning out the lights and going back to kissing in the dark, but I'm hungry. I should have eaten more of Patsy's shrimp.'

'I'm starved,' Theresa said. 'Maybe we could find a candle, turn out the lights, and go in the end of the kitchen away from the window and make some sandwiches. That should be safe enough.'

While they followed Theresa's plan, they discussed the possible plans of attack that the Brimstone brothers might use.

'They might not be going to take a shot at me in here,' Luke pointed out. 'They might have one come in through the front door, and when I try to escape out the back, the other one would be waiting to nail me.'

'Or they might try to overpower you and get you into a car so they could dispose of you somewhere far away,' Theresa said, shuddering at the thought. 'Just because we haven't seen them with a car, it doesn't mean they couldn't rent one.'

'Well, whatever they do,' Luke said, fixing Theresa with an intently serious look, 'I want you to stay out of the way and out of sight. This is my problem. No heroics. Do you understand?'

'Yes, Luke,' Theresa said, pretending meek submission. And, she thought, if you think I'm going to let anything happen to you without doing my best to prevent it, you're crazy.

When they had finished their sandwiches, Luke snuffed out the candle. 'Shall we curl up on one of those cushions and kiss the time away?' he asked, putting his arm around Theresa.

'I don't think we'd be very alert if we did,' Theresa replied. 'However...' as Luke stopped and kissed her in the middle of the living-room, 'maybe we could pull one of the cushions near the french doors and keep an eye on the street.'

'Good idea,' Luke agreed. He pushed aside several plants and tugged one of the giant cushions into position, then held out his arms to Theresa. 'Let's get comfortable. This could be a long night.'

'They might not even come tonight,' Theresa said as she snuggled against Luke on the cushion. 'Maybe they were planning something for tomorrow.'

'I thought of that,' Luke said, finding Theresa's lips with a brief kiss. 'Do you suppose we could arrange for food to be brought in so we don't have to move?'

'Why not?' Theresa said, putting her arms behind Luke's neck and pulling his head down to hers. She kissed him thoroughly, letting her hands begin to explore his broad chest.

'No, no,' Luke said, catching one hand and holding it fast. 'Only kissing. I don't want to be caught literally with my pants down.'

Theresa giggled and then shook her head. 'I don't know what's got into me tonight. I'm not behaving sensibly at all.' She turned and looked up at Luke in the dim, shadowy light filtering in from the street. He was looking at her and smiling, as if he knew the answer to her question. 'Why do I have the feeling that you're one jump ahead of me?' she asked.

'Because I am,' he replied, the whiteness of his teeth gleaming as he laughed softly. 'Because I know that my job is just this far . . .' he held up two fingers, very close together, 'from being done.'

'Oh, dear, that job again,' Theresa said. She sighed and leaned her head against Luke's shoulder. His so-called job must have something to do with what she was doing. She was being what he had called cuddly and lovable. What was it that she was almost, but not quite, doing? Obviously, it didn't mean making love, for he had ruled that out. There was something she was still missing. 'Can't you give me just a little clue?' she asked.

Luke was silent for a long time. 'All right,' he said at last, lying back and looking up at the ceiling, 'I'll give you a very good clue. Suppose we are just as we are, but this cushion is a raft, afloat in the ocean. We've been on it for days, cast adrift when our ship went down. We're out of food and water. The end is near for both of us. Our lips are so dry, our throats so parched, that we can no longer speak. We find, among our remaining provisions, a marking pen with which we can write one last message to tell each other some one thing we had meant to say. What would you write?' He turned and watched Theresa's face intently.

Theresa studied Luke's face, his cheekbones accented by an angular shaft of light from the street, his deep-set eyes so bright and warm they seemed to illuminate the space between them. But there was a tension about his mouth, a faint creasing about his eyes, as if her answer was very important, and he was not quite sure what it would be. But, she thought, as she looked at his dear face and imagined herself on that raft with him, she knew very well what she would write. It was, after all, what she should be telling him now, even though she was still a little afraid. But would he write the same thing?

'I love you,' she answered huskily. 'What would you write?' She felt an almost unbearable tension as Luke's eyes filled with tears, even though he was now smiling. Then suddenly he pulled her into his arms and buried his face in her soft hair.

'Oh, Theresa, my darling, I love you so dearly,' he whispered. His mouth found its way to hers, his passion so intense and reckless now that Theresa gasped at the knowledge of how much he had been holding back before. His hands explored her body, frenzied messages of desire colliding with the deep satisfaction of knowing how much he cared. 'I love you, I love you, I love you,' he murmured as his lips created a fiery path along the trail of bare skin which his eager hands revealed. Theresa answered with the same words, lost in a longing so intense that she was aware only of Luke's lips against her skin, teasing the peaks of her breasts, his tongue tickling her navel. When he turned to pin her beneath him, she revelled in the pulsing movements of his hard, male arousal against her. Her hands clutched at his back, as if to hold him close would make him a part of her forever. Then, very abruptly, he pulled away and looked into her eyes, his mouth drawn into an anguished grimace.

'Not now, Theresa,' he said. 'We can't. This still isn't the right time.' He rolled away and sat up, burying his face in his hands. 'I didn't think it would happen this fast,' he muttered.

Theresa pulled down her sweater and sat up, shaken. 'Damn those Brimstones!' she cried. 'When they show up, I'm going to tear them apart!'

'No, Theresa,' Luke said, 'I don't want you to...'
He stopped, listening intently. 'I thought I heard
something. Do you see anything outside?'

'Oh, lord,' Theresa said, looking out the window.
'There's a black car out in front, right behind Patsy's
car. It wasn't there before we...' She paused and
turned her head, frowning. There was a faint, metallic sound outside the front door. 'It sounds like
someone working the door lock,' she whispered.
'Luke! What are you doing?' Luke had stood up and
started toward the door. He stopped and looked back
at her.

'Be quiet and stay there,' he ordered sternly,
pointing a finger at her. He reached for the doorknob.

'Are you insane?' Theresa leaped to her feet just
as Luke jerked the door open.

One of the Brimstone brothers lurched through the
door, momentarily startled. He quickly recovered and
pulled a gun from his pocket.

'Nice welcome, Thorndike,' he said coolly. 'Let's
go. We're taking you for a ride.'

CHAPTER SEVEN

WITH one swift move, Theresa kicked the gun from the Brimstone's hand. Before he could recover from his surprise, she brought her hand down with all her strength in a chopping motion at the point where his neck met his shoulder. His knees buckled and he fell to the floor with an 'Ooof' sound and lay still.

'That's enough, Theresa!' Luke barked as she contemplated what further damage she might do. He flipped on the lights and knelt beside the fallen Brimstone, who was beginning to blink dazedly. 'You all right, Wilber?' he asked. When the man started to push himself up, staring around wildly, he added, 'It's OK, Wilber. The game's over.'

Theresa froze, while around her the world seemed to whirl, rearranging itself like a kaleidoscope. 'Game? What game?' she demanded shrilly.

'Oh, hello, Miss Long,' Wilber said, apparently noticing her for the first time. He rubbed his neck and grimaced. 'For a lady, you really pack some wallop.'

'What game?' Theresa demanded again. She stared at Luke in disbelief. 'Do you mean,' she said, her voice growing louder with every word, 'that there never was any real threat on your life? It was all a game?'

Luke got to his feet and helped Wilber Brimstone up. 'Just try to keep calm, love,' he said, giving

Theresa a sideways glance. 'I'll explain it all when Wilber's gone.'

'Keep calm?' Theresa exploded. 'You snake! You insidious, dishonest, creepy snake! I should have known you couldn't be trusted.' Tears welling in her eyes, she stared at Luke. 'How could you?'

'Sweetheart,' Luke said, coming toward her, his arms outstretched. 'I love you. That was no illusion. I only wanted...'

'Don't touch me!' Theresa cried. 'Don't come near me! I hate you. I never want to see you again!' She looked frantically about. She had to get out of here, get away from Luke, before he led her off into some other fantasy world where her mind ceased to function and her heart again betrayed her. She spotted Patsy's keys beside the telephone and her bag lying on the floor beside an azalea plant. Without another word, she picked them up and ran out the door. She heard Luke calling after her, 'Wait, Theresa! Come back!'

William Brimstone popped out of the black car. 'Where do you think you're going?' he said gruffly.

'The game's over, William,' Theresa said, shaking her head at him. 'Go ask Wilber and Luke.'

As she slipped into Patsy's flashy sports car, she saw William chugging up the walk to Luke's apartment. She was just pulling away from the kerb when she looked back and saw all three men running for the black car. A hysterical sob escaped her throat. They were going to chase her! Luke's crazy melodrama was still continuing. Well, at least she had the right car for the job, she thought grimly, feeling the powerful surge of the car as she accelerated, and the tightly controlled steering as she took a corner at high speed. The streets were almost deserted. Every time she saw headlights appear in her rear-view mirror, she turned and then turned again, the tyres screeching in complaint at her frantic recklessness. After what seemed like a hundred turns, she looked back. She had finally lost them.

'Good lord, I wonder where I am,' Theresa muttered to herself. Nothing looked familiar. A sign indicated that she would find Interstate 10 East straight ahead. A short time later she was on the wide, deserted highway, heading into the lightening sky of early dawn.

With a heavy sigh, Theresa put the car into cruise control and leaned back, flexing her fingers which had been clenched around the steering wheel until the joints ached. She felt as if she had escaped from one unreal world into another which was even less real. Inside, she felt a terrible, aching emptiness, empty of love and devoid of tears. Around her on the outside was a luxurious car which did not belong to her, driving down a highway to nowhere. She could not keep going, but what else could she do? What must she do next? Her mind refused to function, images of Luke flitting past her tired eyes like visions in a dream, seemingly no more real. And so she drove on, across the Lake Ponchartrain bridge, past the town of Slidell. She slowed as a huge truck pulled on ahead of her at an crossroads, then glanced in the mirror again as something bright attracted her eyes. It was the flashing lights of a police car.

The car pulled along side, and the officer motioned for her to pull over. Now what? Theresa wondered. She had not been driving too fast. She pulled off on

to the shoulder of the road and stopped, then opened
the window and poked her head out. The officer was
approaching her very cautiously, his gun drawn.

'Step out of the car, please, with your hands up,'
he said, 'and then put your hands on top of the car.'

Numbly, Theresa did as she was told. This was only
fitting, she thought. The world had gone mad around
her.

'Where's your identification?' the officer asked,
after frisking Theresa more thoroughly than she
thought necessary.

'My bag. On the seat,' she replied.

The officer eyed her suspiciously. 'Don't move,' he
said, as he reached inside for her bag.

Theresa did not answer. She did not want to talk
to this man. He was one of them. One of those crea-
tures from some other planet, sent here only to be-
devil her. She watched stolidly as he found her purse,
opened it, saw who and what she was, and then gave
her a nasty smile.

'Well, well,' he said. 'A private detective and a car
thief. Very interesting. You're under arrest, Miss
Long.'

So that was it, Theresa thought, as the officer read
her her rights. It wasn't really very interesting or sur-
prising. Luke had reported Patsy's car stolen so that
she would be stopped. Or Patsy had. It didn't matter.
She got silently into the officer's car, ignoring his
comments on how quiet she was. Maybe, she thought
as she leaned back and closed her eyes, she could go
to sleep and wake up to find out that this whole night
had been only a bad dream.

When Theresa opened her eyes again, it was daylight and the officer was urging her from the police car. Some dream, she thought grimly as she was ushered into a large, official-looking building, put through the necessary procedures involved in being charged with car theft, and then left staring through the bars of a gaol cell. She had used her one telephone call to call Quentin and ask him to track down a good local lawyer for her. Quent, bless his heart, had assumed there was a reason for what she had done, even though she only told him that she would explain everything later. How long, she wondered, as she sat down on the narrow prison bunk and leaned her chin in her hand, would she have to be in gaol? Even now, nothing seemed quite real. It didn't seem possible that Luke could have played such a miserable trick on her. He had trapped her, peeled her defences away, and . . .

Tears started to trickle from Theresa's eyes. She wiped them away and clenched her teeth. She wasn't going to cry and make an even bigger fool of herself. That would serve no useful purpose. She was going to wait until a few days had passed, then think the whole thing over calmly and rationally. Without Luke around to bother her, she ought to be able to do that again. Meanwhile, she might as well go back to sleep and see if she could get rid of the throbbing ache that extended from her head clear to her knotted calf muscles. She curled up on the bunk and closed her eyes.

The clanking of her cell being opened awakened Theresa.

'C'mon out,' said the gaoler with a friendly smile. 'You've been sprung.'

'By whom?' Theresa asked, getting groggily to her feet and following him.

'Fellow named Thorndike,' the gaoler answered.

'Oh, no!' Theresa cried. Quent must have called him. She should have explained what had happened! She felt like running back to the cell, but it was too late. Luke was waiting for her by the duty officer's desk, holding her bag. He said nothing, merely cocking one eyebrow at her and taking a firm hold of her arm. He still said nothing when he put her into that same black car which had pursued her the previous night. When he had taken his place behind the wheel, he looked over at her.

'Well?' he asked.

'Well, what?' Theresa snapped. 'If you mean where do I want to go, certainly not back to your apartment.'

'Don't you want to know how I found you?' Luke smiled crookedly. 'That was quite a chase last night, but I didn't expect you to head for the border.'

'I assumed that Quentin called you,' Theresa said, staring out the front window. 'Didn't you turn in the car as stolen?'

'No, Patsy did, but I didn't know it until Quentin called. I've persuaded her to drop the charges,' Luke replied.

'Wonderful,' Theresa said coldly. 'I don't know when I've been so thrilled. Take me to a hotel. Any hotel.'

'Theresa,' Luke growled, starting the car and moving into the traffic, 'I don't see how you can so completely misinterpret everything. Haven't you thought about it at all?'

'I don't want to think about it,' she replied. 'I want to forget it. I want to forget you! Where are we going?'

'Back to my apartment,' Luke answered. 'In case you've forgotten, all of your things are there. I'm not going to bring them to you somewhere else, so you'll have to come and get them. And while we're there, we're going to have a little talk. After that, if you still want to leave, you may. But I'm warning you, you'll never get rid of me. I'll follow you to the ends of the earth if I have to, until I can beat some sense into that head of yours.'

'Sense? Into my head? That would be a novelty,' Theresa said sarcastically. 'All you've ever done is knock all the sense out of it. I'm not going to let that happen to me again.'

Luke gave her a disgusted look, but said nothing more until they were back at his apartment.

'Now, then,' he said, keeping a painfully tight grip on her arm until he had deposited her in a chair by the kitchen table, 'let's see how sensible you really are. First of all, what would you do if you loved somebody desperately, but they'd sworn they never wanted to see you again? And I'm talking about the first time you said that, not last night. Would you just give up?'

'The first time? You claim you loved me desperately then?' Theresa watched Luke nod, her mouth pursed in a disbelieving line. 'I certainly wouldn't wait five years to do something about it,' she said scathingly. 'That doesn't do much for the credibility of your devotion. In fact, I think it's an out and out lie.'

'Stop that, Theresa,' Luke said warningly. 'I don't lie. I never told you that I wasn't married, and I never made any promises to you that I couldn't keep.'

'Then what took you so long?' Theresa demanded. 'Did your wife have so much on you that you were afraid she'd take everything in a divorce settlement?'

Luke leaned forward, his brows drawn together menacingly. 'Theresa, stop acting like such a shrew. I'm losing patience with you. She had nothing on me, because there was nothing to have. Sonya was an alcoholic. I stayed with her for three miserable years in the hope I could do some good. I couldn't. The divorce took a long time to arrange, because I wanted things set up so she couldn't drink and gamble away everything in a few months' time and wind up a pauper, and she wanted everything at once.'

Theresa frowned. 'Funny you never got around to telling me all that before.'

'When did you ever give me a chance?' Luke thundered. 'Besides,' he said, lowering his voice, 'it wasn't something I cared to drag you into early on. I didn't want to string you along with that old line about divorcing my wife some day, because it might not have been true. If staying would have helped Sonya, I probably would have, in spite of everything. I don't abandon people who need me.' A small spark appeared in the dark depths of his eyes. 'Which is why I won't abandon you.'

'Whatever gave you the illusion that I need you?' Theresa asked coldly. 'I was doing very well until you popped back into my life. Does the fact that you're capable of arousing me sexually add up to need in that warped mind of yours?'

Luke's lips tightened. 'I do believe we'd got past the mere issue of sex. You told me that you love me.'

'Temporary insanity,' Theresa said, trying to ignore the ache inside that remembering that moment caused. 'I got carried away by your story of the life raft. I'm a sucker for sad dog stories, too.' She pushed her chair back and stood up. 'Now, whether you like it or not, I'm going to gather up my things and get out of here.'

'All right,' Luke said with a sigh, 'but you'll be back. It would save a lot of time and trouble if you'd stay.'

'Not a chance,' Theresa said coldly. She went to find her suitcase, and then started putting her clothing into it.

'You haven't given me a chance to explain about the twins,' Luke said, leaning against the bedroom door-frame and watching her. 'I think you owe it to me to listen to what I have to say, since you've obviously over-reacted in entirely the wrong way.'

'I'm not interested,' Theresa said, sending him an angry glance. 'No one likes being made a fool of.'

'I'm the fool,' Luke said quietly. 'It wasn't a game, Theresa, not to me. I wanted you near me, to give us a chance to get back to what we had five years ago. Since I tend to think in stories, I thought of one which might bring you close. I thought that if you still cared about me, learning that my life was in danger would do that.'

'But you never thought about how I'd feel when I found out I'd been tricked? I don't think you know me very well, Luke. Not very well at all.' She zipped her suitcase shut. 'Call a taxi for me, please,' she said. 'I'm ready to leave.' She started for the door, but stopped when Luke did not move. For some reason, the idea of getting too close to him made her feel shaky inside, and the way he was watching her through sad, thoughtful eyes created an uncomfortable turbulence in her heart. She set her chin and scowled, more at herself than Luke. Even after what he'd done, did her body have no more sense than that? Why in the devil couldn't it get better co-ordinated with her mind? 'Would you mind?' she snapped impatiently. 'I can't get through.'

'Don't be in such a rush,' Luke said. 'I'll take you where you want to go. I was just thinking that things would probably have gone better if my story hadn't climaxed so soon. It's difficult controlling the outcome when you have live actors ad libbing as they go along. I think I was generally on the right track, though. I do know you, Theresa, better than you know yourself. I know that you really do love me, but you're still very much afraid of the commitment that implies. The smallest thing makes you jump back behind your protective shield of denial. I'll just have to take things a little slower from here on.'

'You aren't going to take anything anywhere,' Theresa said, irritated that his words made even the slightest sense to her. 'If I didn't have to stay in New Orleans to try and track down that idiot Toby McDonald, I'd be a thousand miles away from here by tomorrow.'

'Oh, yes,' Luke said, finally moving aside, 'McDonald. I'd almost forgotten about him. You never mentioned what luck you had yesterday. Did you find Carmelita?'

'None of your business,' Theresa snapped. She reached for the telephone. Luke was not going to worm his way into that affair by being helpful. She would do it alone, or not at all.

'Mmm. No luck, huh?' Luke said. He reached over and took the telephone from Theresa's hand. 'I said I'd take you wherever you're going,' he said firmly. 'But first, tell me what happened yesterday. You must have learned something. No good detective could spend four hours tramping the streets without getting some information.'

'No!' Theresa said, her chin jutting belligerently. 'It's none of your business, and it's going to stay that way.' She picked up her suitcase and edged toward the door. 'Get out of my way, Luke. If you won't call me a taxi, I'll walk.'

'No, you won't,' Luke said, pinning her against the door with a hand on either side of her. 'And you're not going to try any karate on me, either,' he said, as her eyes narrowed dangerously. 'You don't really want to leave my poor, mangled body lying on the floor. And you do really want to have my help tracking down Toby McDonald. Now, tell me what you know. You aren't going anywhere until you do.'

Theresa glared at him, her chest rising and falling heavily from the suffocating warmth that having him so close produced. For a moment she had the mad notion that he had some kind of supernatural power that enabled him to lure her into a vortex of emotion, like a vacuum cleaner sucking up wisps of dust. But he didn't. Not really. If she kept her head, she could neutralise his powers. Then she could be free of him once and for all.

'I won't tell you anything,' she said defiantly.

'We could be here a long time,' Luke replied. He smiled slowly, his eyes wandering down to Theresa's lips. His tongue flicked his lower lip suggestively. 'This isn't such a bad position, is it? I could kiss you.' He looked back into Theresa's eyes, devilish sparks in his own. 'But I won't. I'm not going to kiss you again for a long time. By the time I get around to it, you'll be begging me to.'

'In a pig's eye, I will,' Theresa snapped, feeling beads of perspiration break out on her upper lip. 'I'll never beg you for anything.'

Luke only smiled and changed the subject. 'Let's see. If you didn't find Carmelita, that can't mean too many different things: number one, she's not here any more and no one knows anything about her; number two, she was here but went off with McDonald to parts unknown; number three, she quit dancing to get married and raise a family, not with McDonald... Aha! I can tell by your face that that's the answer. So Carmelita's out of the picture, and God only knows where else McDonald might be. Right?'

I can't be that transparent, Theresa thought desperately, feeling another wave of supernatural-like anxiety sweeping through her. She clenched her hands, trying to regain some semblance of calm. It was only a lucky guess on Luke's part. That was all it was.

'So the next question is,' Luke went on, frowning thoughtfully, 'what is McDonald apt to be doing? He was a jazz buff, as I recall. He could just be hanging around the clubs, drinking himself into a stupor over

losing Carmelita. Or he might have taken up with
another dancer. Some fellows really go for that type
of woman. Do you have a picture of the guy? It would
help when we go around to show it to people.'

Theresa felt like screaming. 'Will you butt out?'
she cried. 'I will find Mr McDonald without your
help.'

Luke shook his head. 'No, you won't. In less time
than it takes to tell, I can spread the word that poor
Toby McDonald's wife, a cute little blonde masquer-
ading as a detective named Theresa Long, is hot on
his trail. The poor guy would do anything to keep
away from her. I'd have everyone feeling so sorry for
him that no one would tell you anything. On the other
hand,' he said, grinning as Theresa groaned, 'if you
accept my help, I'll bet we can find him within a week.'

I will not let this get to me, Theresa told herself,
fighting off another wave of desperation. Look on
the bright side. If you finish the case, you can get out
of here. 'Good,' she said. 'I'll be only too glad to
finish the case and get back to Chicago. When do we
begin?'

'That's better,' Luke said. 'One small step forward.
I guess, since you're so determined to leave, I should
take you to a hotel. The Royal Orleans will do. We
can have some dinner there, and then start hitting the
clubs. There are dozens, so it may take a while.'

Theresa opened her mouth to protest and then
closed it again. Let Luke think that he was running
the show. She'd find some way to give him the slip
and do things her own way. Of course, Luke was right
about showing the picture of Toby McDonald to
people. She'd already thought of that. Too bad it was

such an old picture. The dancers had said that he was fat and balding now. You would think that someone who claimed to love her husband as much as Mrs McDonald did would have taken his picture some time in the last five years.

She let Luke take her to the Royal Orleans, but she refused to let him see her to her room.

'Wait right there,' she told him, pointing to a comfortable chair in the lobby. 'I'll be back as soon as I'm ready for dinner.' Or maybe she wouldn't. If there was some other way out...

CHAPTER EIGHT

THERESA flung her suitcase on the bed in the luxurious hotel room and then slumped down beside it. She felt exhausted. It was not, she knew, only from lack of sleep. Being near Luke Thorndike and fighting the tentacles of the web he tried to weave was exhausting. He'd kept watching her while she'd registered for her room, his lips curved into a little smile, his eyes dark and deep and warm. She had the feeling that, even though she was now alone in her room, he was still watching, which might not be such a paranoid thought. It had occurred to her that he must have had someone watching her for a long time. How else would he have known when she was going to take the train to New Orleans? It couldn't have been a coincidence, not with the Brimstone brothers on the same train. He had known about Carl Weidenkamp, too. Did he really know Carl's boss, or had some detective he'd hired told him? Was Luke, in fact, the victim of some deranged fixation on her? She had once met a woman who was pursued by a man like that. She couldn't stand the sight of him, but he kept insisting that she really loved him but didn't realise it.

Her case was not exactly parallel, Theresa admitted to herself as she shook out her clothes and hung them in the closet. Luke made her furious, but it was what he had done, not the sight of him, she hated. She really felt a little bit sorry for him. He thought he

understood her, when he really didn't understand her
at all. If he'd just come to Chicago and asked her out
instead of going through his ridiculous charade, things
might have turned out differently. He could have explained about his wife, and she would have understood. And, in time, if he'd acted like a normal human
being, she might have learned to trust him.

That was the trouble, Theresa thought with a sigh.
Luke wasn't a normal human being. He was a gifted
and creative writer. Were all writers as crazy as he
was? If so, their wives must have to be a very understanding lot. Maybe poor Sonya hadn't been able to
take it. Maybe Luke had driven her to drink! It was
a good thing for one Theresa Long that she was on
to his tricks now, or she could have ended up in the
same situation. Not that Luke had ever mentioned
marriage.

Theresa showered and put on a severely simple black
dress and matching jacket. It would keep her from
standing out in a crowd, making it harder for Luke
to find her. Now to find another way out of this hotel.
Wouldn't Luke be surprised when he discovered she
was gone! Smiling to herself at the thought, she
opened the door. Her smile faded.

'You look lovely,' Luke said, from his position,
leaning against the wall opposite her room. He grinned
at her downcast expression. 'I was afraid you might
try to sneak out on me. Of course, that thought never
entered your mind, did it?'

'Oh, it did,' Theresa said icily. 'That, and several
other less pleasant ways of disposing of you.' Luke's
chuckle at her remark was infuriating. It was time he
realised that she was not joking about getting away

from him. Maybe if she spelled it out for him one more time, he would begin to get the picture. 'Don't be so jolly,' she said. 'I'll get rid of you yet. And if I can't shake you in New Orleans, I can cling to the thought that I'll soon be back in Chicago, without you.'

'Maybe a good dinner will help you to stop hallucinating,' Luke said, giving her another little smile. 'You seem to have forgotten that I promised you I'd follow you to the ends of the earth, and Chicago isn't even half-way there. The point is, Terry, love,' he added, as angry sparks flared in her eyes, 'that you might as well begin to accept my presence in your life. I'm not going to try any more dramatic tricks to get you there. I'll simply be there, waiting for you to stop bridling like a rambunctious horse, and admit you meant it when you said you loved me.'

'You'll be old and grey before that,' Theresa snapped.

'So will you, my love, so will you,' Luke replied calmly. 'And we will have grown old together.'

There was no point in discussing that topic any further, Theresa realised grimly. Luke simply didn't listen. She kept determinedly silent while he led her to one of the elegant restaurants in the hotel and ordered that champagne he brought, although what he thought there might be to celebrate at the moment she couldn't imagine and was afraid to ask.

When the cork had been popped and their glasses filled, he raised his. 'To the most beautiful woman in the world,' he said. 'Any moment that I can spend with her is worth celebrating with the finest champagne.' He smiled at her across the top of his glass, and Theresa felt a strange quivering in her stomach.

That was, she thought, a beautiful thing to say, especially since she had spent the day acting like a shrew, or worse. And unfortunately, no matter what other things he might have said or done to deceive her, she did not doubt that he meant it.

'Thank you,' she said tightly, taking a sip of her own champagne. It was, as he had said, very fine. The dinner, too, was elegant and expensive. Vowing to herself that she was going to regain the upper hand and not let herself be obligated to Luke for anything further, Theresa insisted on adding the dinner expenses to her room tab.

'The A-1 Detective Agency will pay for it,' she told Luke when he tried to protest. 'And, since you insist on taking part in my current case, you may now consider yourself one of our employees. That means you take orders from me, not the other way around.'

Luke rubbed his chin thoughtfully. 'Does that mean you're not going to try to get away from me again?' he asked, an annoying twinkle in his eyes.

'Yes, it does,' Theresa replied. 'It also means that I am going to use you as effectively as possible. For the rest of this evening, I want you to interview as many of the show girls as you can, on the chance that one of them has been approached recently by our Mr McDonald. I'm sure they'll be more willing to talk to you than they would to me. Meanwhile, I'm going to start checking out the bartenders and musicians in this area.'

'Who will doubtless be happier to talk to you,' Luke said drily. 'I hope you have more than one picture of

McDonald. After all, he might have used a different name so that his wife couldn't trace him.'

'That's right,' Theresa agreed. 'I have only one picture, but we can fix that easily. We'll stop at the hotel desk and ask them to make a copy of it for us. I'm sure they won't mind.' When she had the copy in hand, she gave Luke the original.

'Rather a nondescript fellow, isn't he?' Luke commented, frowning at the picture of a man holding a trumpet.

'I'm afraid so,' Theresa agreed, 'but that's all his wife had. He's also several years older and heavier now. It may be more useful to mention that the trumpet used to belong to Louis Armstrong. From what his wife said, he brags about it a lot. I'll bet he couldn't spend an evening with a girl without mentioning it.' And, she thought, she would bet he couldn't talk to anyone in one of the jazz clubs for five minutes without mentioning his trumpet.

'All right, I'll check out the girls,' Luke said, when they had once again reached Bourbon Street, 'but why don't you wait until I've finished that to start on the clubs? I'd feel better if you didn't go prowling around at night, unescorted.' He smiled beguilingly. 'Please?'

Theresa shook her head, steeling herself against the warm, cosy feeling that his concern tried to start in her heart. His kind of concern, she told herself sternly, she did not need.

'I can take care of myself,' she reminded him. 'The idea is to bring this case to a conclusion as quickly as possible. Having the two of us pursue different aspects of the case is more efficient. You can call me in the morning and tell me what you found out.'

Luke looked down at the picture, then smiled, casting a mischievous glance at Theresa from beneath his long lashes. 'I'll come over and we'll have breakfast together,' he said. 'I may even see you later this evening. Don't get the idea that you can order me out of your life, Terry, love. It won't work.' With that, he gave her a wink and walked off, whistling to himself.

Theresa watched him for a moment, feeling strangely unsettled, then deliberately turned her back on him. Don't let him get to you, she reminded herself. Keep the upper hand. Ignore his threats. Just do your job, and do it well. She straightened her shoulders and took off at a brisk pace toward the first doorway, through which the sweet, soulful sounds of a jazz combo were floating.

She took a seat on a bar stool, and struck up a conversation with the bartender, explaining her mission. Her heart sank when he told her that someone was always claiming they had a trumpet that used to belong to Louis Armstrong.

'Or Al Hirt,' he added. 'And I suppose now that having one that belonged to Wynton Marsalis is the big thing. Poor suckers buy some old battered thing from some guy in a dark alley. I don't know if they really believe it or just want to impress people.' He peered at Theresa's picture. 'Doesn't look like especially like anyone I've seen lately,' he said. 'But he's kind of average-looking, you know what I mean?'

'I'm afraid I do,' Theresa replied with a sigh.

'Don't get discouraged,' the bartender advised sympathetically. 'He'll turn up. Why don't you stick around and ask the boys when they finish their set?

Might as well get everyone on the alert.' He grinned, showing a gold tooth in the front. 'Don't hurt to have such a pretty girl hunting for the fellow, now does it?'

Theresa waited to talk to the musicians, having to spend part of her time actively discouraging a man who came to sit next to her and wanted to buy her a drink. When she did talk to the musicians, none of them had any information about Toby McDonald. She left her card with the bartender, in case anyone did hear of the man, and went on down the street.

It was the same story at the next club, although Theresa thought the music there was a bit better.

'I'll get to be a regular jazz connoisseur,' she muttered to herself as she left. It took an inordinate amount of time, waiting for the musicians to have a break, and then having long enough conversations with everyone so that she felt they really would call her if they found out something about Toby. At this rate, she'd be lucky to get through another two clubs before midnight. She was just gathering her wits to start into another smoke-filled café when a large, burly man with a cigar clenched between his teeth came up behind her and put an arm around her shoulders.

'Hello, cutie,' he said, peering into her face and grinning, showing teeth yellowed from his smoking habit. 'I saw you down the street. You looking for someone special to keep you company tonight?'

Theresa gave him an icy stare. 'No, I'm not,' she replied. 'I'm a private detective, looking for a missing man. Unless your name is Toby McDonald, I'm not looking for you.'

'You're kidding me,' the man said, grinning even more broadly as Theresa shook her head. 'Hey, that's real neat, little lady. If I was missing, I sure would like you to come and find me. Why don't you just come along and have a little drink with me, and tell me all about it? I'll just bet I can help you. I read a lot of detective stories.'

'I have to talk to some people in this club right now,' Theresa said, trying to maintain her composure. She did not want to have to resort to force in order to rid herself of this pest. 'The man I'm looking for is a real jazz fan. They may have seen him.'

That statement got the man moving into the club, although Theresa would have liked to see him go another direction. He sat down next to her at the bar, breathing bourbon-laden breath in her direction, and interjecting unhelpful comments into her discussion with the bartender. He followed her when, after another unsuccessful discussion, she started to leave.

'Look, Mr...'

'Thompson. Orville Thompson,' the man furnished. 'Where to next, Theresa?' He had picked up her name when she'd told the bartender.

'Mr Thompson, I think I'll just check one more club tonight.' She looked at her watch. 'It's getting late. Don't you have a wife who's waiting for you, like Mr McDonald's poor wife is doing?' She had noticed that the man wore a wedding ring.

'Oh, no, ma'am,' Orville replied. 'My wife's dead and gone.' He held up his hand and looked at the ring. 'Darn thing's stuck on. Too tight to get off. They say they could cut it off, but somehow I feel like it's a sign, you know? Means Millie is still with me, in spirit.'

'That's...a nice thought,' Theresa said with a sigh. And she, apparently, was stuck with Orville unless she got really nasty. For the first time that evening, she began to wish that Luke was with her. She wished so even more when Orville followed her as she left the club, still none the wiser about Toby McDonald.

'I do think you ought to come and have a little nightcap with me,' Orville persisted, clutching at Theresa's arm. 'We might even get into something more serious. I may not look it, but I've got plenty of money. Plenty of money. Own my own garage back in Dubuque, Iowa.'

Theresa stopped and jerked her arm free. 'Mr Thompson,' she snapped, 'I have been very patient with you, but I want you to go away and leave me alone. I am not available!'

'And I've been pretty patient with you,' Orville growled, his expression suddenly threatening. He grabbed Theresa's arm again in a vice-like grip. 'Now, just you come along with me real quiet like. I want to buy you a little drink. That isn't too much to ask, is it?'

You've asked for it, Theresa thought to herself grimly, every muscle now tense and poised for action. She was mentally measuring the time to make her move, when suddenly Luke stepped in front of them.

'Let go of the lady,' he said quietly. 'She belongs to me.'

'Sez who?' Orville repeated belligerently, dropping Theresa's arm and assuming a threatening pose in front of Luke.

Oh, lord, Theresa thought, that's all I need now. Luke and Orville in a street brawl. Quickly she said, 'Orville, he is my fiancé, and I wouldn't mess with him if I were you. He's a karate champion. Maybe you've heard of him. Luke Thorndike?'

Orville dropped his clenched fists. 'Oh, yeah,' he said. 'Thorndike.' He looked over at Theresa, and then back at Luke. 'Where the hell have you been while she's been out looking for that McDonald guy? Seems you could be more help.' He scowled again at Luke and then nodded at Theresa. 'Good luck, Theresa. If I hear anything, I'll let you know.'

After he had gone, Theresa looked up at Luke. 'Where do you get that "she belongs to me" line?' she demanded. 'Couldn't you just have told Orville to let go of me without that?'

Luke smiled slowly. 'I love you, and you love me. I think that adds up to you belonging to me,' he said. 'You did look very glad to see me.' His eyes twinkled mischievously. 'Or were you just playing hard to get with Orville?'

'Of course not,' Theresa said stiffly, her tense nerves tingling with a new and different warmth. 'But I could have taken care of Orville myself. I was just about to.'

'Theresa,' Luke caught her chin and lifted it toward him, searching her face with eyes now deeply serious, 'can't you at least admit that you were glad to see me?'

Theresa looked past Luke. Upstairs, across the street, in the light of a window behind an iron-railed balcony filled with flowers, she could see a man and woman kissing. An aching tightness made her voice almost inaudible. 'Yes, I was glad,' she replied, turning her eyes back to Luke's. When he smiled again, the ache moved to her heart. She did not even protest when he put his arm around her as they started walking down the street.

Nor did she complain when he said, 'In case you wondered, I've been watching and waiting for you since I saw Orville follow you into the last two clubs you visited. You were never in any danger. Did you have any luck on McDonald?'

'No,' Theresa said with a sigh. 'Did you?'

'Nope. I did find out that a lot of guys think they have one of Louis Armstrong's old trumpets.'

'Me, too,' Theresa said, wondering why, at the moment, she did not even care. Was it because she was so tired, and Luke's strong arm around her made her feel so safe? Or was it that nagging little feeling somewhere inside that seemed to be trying to tell her that there was something more important to her than Toby McDonald and his trumpet?

Luke took Theresa to the door of her room. 'You look so tired, love,' he said, gently caressing her hair back from her forehead. 'Why don't you sleep in in the morning? There's not much we can do until afternoon, anyway. We could have brunch at about eleven.'

'All right,' Theresa said numbly. She had felt herself leaning more and more heavily against Luke as they walked along. Her eyes were burning from fatigue and the smoke of the nightclubs. She gave Luke a faint smile. 'I'll see you at eleven, then. Where?'

'Right here,' Luke replied. He let one finger trace along her cheek, then follow the curve of her lips.

'Sleep well, Terry, love,' he said. He backed away. 'Goodnight. Be sure and lock your door tight.'

'Aren't...' she began, then closed her mouth, rubbed her hand across her eyes and shook her head. 'Goodnight, Luke,' she said, hurriedly opening her door and going inside. Without even taking off her shoes, she flung herself face down on her bed and clutched desperately at her pillow. What was wrong with her? She had almost asked Luke if he wasn't going to kiss her goodnight! Was it happening to her again, in spite of everything?

When Theresa awoke, she could not even remember having put on her pyjamas, and it took her several seconds to realise where she was and that the telephone was ringing.

'Hello?' she croaked hoarsely.

'Theresa, what's going on?' demanded Quentin's voice. 'Luke told me you got mad at him, then drove off in the neighbour's car, and now you're staying at a hotel. Are you all right? You sound terrible.'

Theresa cleared her throat. 'Yes, I'm fine,' she answered, her mind finally beginning to function. 'Did Luke tell you why I was angry? *Am* angry?' At Quentin's negative reply, she poured out the whole story. Expecting heartfelt sympathy from her brother, she let go the tears that had not come before at Luke's treachery. Instead, he sounded almost as if he sided with Luke.

'Now, Theresa,' he said, 'I do think you're being a little melodramatic. It was rather unorthodox, but after all, it's not every woman who has a man willing to go to such lengths to get her attention. I should think you'd be flattered.'

'Flattered?' Theresa cried, still sniffling. 'How can you . . . Oh, never mind!' Men! How they did all stick together. She discussed her thus far fruitless search for Toby McDonald with her brother, securing his promise to check back with the man's wife to see if she'd had any further ideas. When she had hung up, she sat cross-legged on her bed and stared disconsolately into space. 'Give it a few more days,' Quentin had said, 'and then come home. We can't win 'em all.' Well, she was going to win this one. And she wasn't going to let Luke Thorndike weaken her defences again. She had been too tired last night, that was all. She hadn't really wanted him to kiss her at all.

Promptly at eleven o'clock, there was a knock at her door.

'Room service,' said a familiar voice.

Frowning curiously, Theresa opened the door.

'Brunch is served, ma'am,' said Luke, entering the room, pushing a trolley before him. 'I thought it would be more pleasant to eat in privacy.' He parked the trolley next to the small table near the windows and smiled at Theresa. 'You're looking lovely, as usual,' he said. 'Blue becomes you.'

Theresa felt her cheeks grow warm. From the moment that Luke had entered the room, she had done nothing but stare at him. Why was it that she could never remember from one time to the next how incredibly handsome he was? In a black turtle-neck sweater and grey trousers, his dark hair gleaming with highlights, he seemed to fill the room with a vibrant electricity.

'Creole omelette,' he said, removing the cover from one of the dishes with a flourish. 'Croissants,' he announced, uncovering the basket. 'Honeydew melon, orange juice, coffee.' He raised one black eyebrow. 'Theresa, are you there?'

'Oh, yes!' She blushed, then cursed herself for doing so and took a deep breath. 'It looks wonderful,' she said, 'but you shouldn't have . . .'

'I know,' Luke interrupted, 'it's less expensive to go out, but we have so much to talk about, and I don't think we'd want anyone to overhear, do you?'

'What on earth are you talking about?' Theresa demanded, taking her place at the table. 'Neither one of us found out anything yesterday to talk about.'

'*Au contraire,*' Luke said. He paused and looked at the croissant he was buttering with an amused smile. 'Why do I always feel like speaking French when I'm eating one of these?' he asked, his eyes twinkling as he looked up at Theresa.

'*Je ne sais pas,*' she answered, unable to resist his good humour, although she could not fathom its source. 'And,' she added, 'I still don't know what this deeply secret conversation of ours is supposed to be about.'

Luke savoured a bit of croissant, took a sip of coffee, seeming to deliberately enjoy making Theresa wait for his answer. At last he leaned toward her and answered, 'Us. You wanted me to kiss you last night. You almost asked me to. I think it's time we beat a retreat to some time before the débâcle with the Brimstone brothers who, incidentally, are great admirers of yours, and started over.'

'I was tired last night,' Theresa said defensively. 'My mind wasn't working. And there's nothing that can erase what you so aptly call the débâcle of the Brimstone brothers. So there's nothing to talk about.'

'Wrong,' said Luke. 'I want you to talk about the Brimstones. Castigate me. Tell me exactly what I did wrong, and why I should never have done it. I obviously need correction, and where else am I to get it? Just pretend that you're a psychiatrist—say, Dr Theresa Longfreud, and I am some poor, confused man named Thorny Lukewarm, who has done to Susie Mae Pickrell exactly what that dastardly Luke Thorndike did to you. Help me, Dr Longfreud. My life is in your hands.'

Theresa gave up trying to keep her twitching lips from smiling. 'Thorny Lukewarm, indeed,' she said. 'You may be thorny, but I don't think anyone would ever accuse you of being lukewarm about anything. Maybe that's one of your problems. You get an idea, and then the idea runs away with you before you think it through. Why didn't you just come to Chicago and knock on my door? I would have invited you in. You could have told me about your ex-wife. I would have understood a lot of things better then.'

Luke took a bite of his omelette and chewed it thoughtfully. 'Excellent omelette,' he said. 'Yes, doctor, I believe there's some merit in what you say,' he went on, 'and I suppose in a year or two you might have come around to deciding that you loved me, after all. But I don't like Chicago that well, and I still don't understand exactly why what I did was so terrible. We had some excitement, some fun, and found our love much more quickly. Even more quickly than I'd hoped. There's nothing phony or deceitful about my love for you. I love you just as much here on dry land as I would on any raft. Could you only imagine loving me if I was about to die?' He raised his eyebrows quizzically at Theresa, waiting for her answer.

Theresa looked away from Luke's probing gaze. He was trying to trap her again. Not this time, he wouldn't! 'I can't imagine loving you at all,' she said stiffly.

'That's a lie, Theresa,' Luke said flatly. 'And you know it. All right, then, answer this. Why did you say you loved me, if it's completely beyond your imagination now? The only difference between then and now is the story I told you, in which case the answer to my question is yes.'

'Oh, stop it, Luke! Just stop it!' Theresa cried. She flung down her napkin and jumped up from her chair. Tears welled in her eyes. 'I don't know why I said it. I guess at the time I meant it. I thought I could trust you, but I can't. You deceived me.'

Luke came to stand in front of her. 'Tell me this, Theresa,' he said, raising her face to his with one finger, 'I thought there was a difference between the kind of deceit involved with a man who cheats on his wife or a father who deserts his family, and the kind of make-believe I engage in. Am I wrong?'

Theresa jerked her head away and rubbed at her teary cheeks. 'You always make things sound so logical. I don't know the answer. I just know how I felt.'

'But,' Luke said, putting his hands on Theresa's shoulders and then sliding them around to her back, 'you like make-believe. And I can't live without it.

I'm a writer, you know. If you truly feel there's no difference, then I guess we should say goodbye, for I can't promise I'd never do anything like that again, and I don't want to make you unhappy. I couldn't bear that.' He pulled Theresa close and laid his cheek against her hair. 'I don't want to say goodbye,' he said, a note that sounded almost like a sob in his voice.

This is it, Theresa thought, standing very still, her heart pounding erratically. This is the chance I've been waiting for to rid myself of Luke Thorndike forever. She could tell that he really meant what he said. All she had to say would be, 'Well, I guess it's goodbye, then.' But did she want to say goodbye? Standing in the circle of Luke's arms, feeling his warmth, the gentleness of his touch, was probably not the time to make such a decision. It made her think of how she felt when he kissed her, how his smile could thrill her to her very toes. Of how special she felt when she shared one of his fantasies, as if they were almost one person, adrift in a world of their own. Was she wrong to feel so hurt at his deception? Logically, she could see his point. But it was so hard to make logic change what she felt. So easy to reject all of the good along with the bad. He had, she remembered, said something about that. The easier negative. Maybe that had been what he meant when he said he had a job to do. He had to teach her to stop looking only at the easier negative, to be able to see that there were other sides to look at. Maybe if she tried harder to count the good points . . .

Feeling so tightly drawn that she would shatter like a dry leaf if Luke were to squeeze her, Theresa slowly let herself lean against him. Poor darling. His heart

was pounding at the sometimes frenetic pace of a jazz
drummer. He was as worried as she was over what
she would decide. Her arms crept around to his broad
back, hard with muscular tension, and, as she
tightened her grip, he tightened his.

'I love you, Theresa,' Luke murmured.

Theresa closed her eyes. If she told Luke goodbye,
she would never hear that again, in his velvet voice,
never feel like this again, so close and secure in his
arms. A nice, calm, orderly, dull life. A life without
the man she loved with such unreasoning passion that
she was even now beginning to tremble with longing
in the midst of her confusion. She raised her head
and saw in his eyes so clearly the loving and longing
that it brought tears to her eyes.

'I love you, too, Luke,' she said huskily. 'I couldn't
bear to say goodbye.'

CHAPTER NINE

TIME stood still, capturing Luke's face in an expression Theresa knew she would remember forever. There was relief, and joy, but most of all love. Then his lips found hers, recalling the hunger and passion of the last time she had told him she loved him. Every vestige of the aching tension that had been building ever since Wilber Brimstone made his unfortunate entrance into Luke's apartment vanished in a sigh of happiness. She closed her eyes and lost herself in a world of nothing but sensations. The taste of Luke's loving mouth, the strength of his passionate embrace, the solid masculinity of his body close to hers. She smiled when he drew away for a moment and smiled at her, then crushed her to him again.

'Lord, I feel so much better,' he said, nibbling his way with a path of kisses from Theresa's mouth to her ear.

'So do I,' she agreed. She angled her chin against his as he returned toward her mouth again, and laid her hand along his cheek. 'I hope I can learn to deal better with your fantasies,' she said. 'I'll try very hard. But do try not to shock me quite so much, will you? Only pleasant surprises.'

Luke smiled wryly. 'I'll do my best, but I can't guarantee the results. I would have sworn you'd find it a pleasant surprise to find that my life wasn't in danger, after all.'

'I guess it should have been,' Theresa admitted. 'I'm a slow learner.' She laced her arms beneath Luke's again and held him close. 'On the other hand, I think there are some things you're a little slow about.'

'Such as?' Luke demanded.

'Well...' Theresa looked over at her bed. 'There's a nice, comfortable bed, and we're not anticipating any visits from the Brimstones this morning.' She looked back at Luke and pressed her hips suggestively against his. 'Twice now you've told me it wasn't the right time. Maybe the third time's the charm?'

Luke took a deep breath and cleared his throat uncomfortably. 'There's something I'd better explain about that. I probably should have before, but somehow it didn't seem appropriate either time.' At Theresa's anxious look, he chuckled. 'No, Terry, love, I'm not impotent. It's just that I have what most of Earthling society would consider a weird hang-up about making love to women I'm not married to. I suppose it's my religious upbringing. That's why I could never have been the philanderer that you imagined, and never will. In your case, the flesh is certainly willing, but I wouldn't feel right about it. Of course, you did tell old Orville last night that we were engaged. So maybe if we were...'

'I also told him that you were a karate champion,' Theresa said, frowning. 'But, if that's a proposal...' A sharp little twinge of fear passed through her. She did love Luke, and certainly respected his feelings about sex outside of marriage, but marriage was such a big, permanent step.

'It is,' Luke said quickly. He smiled at Theresa's worried look. 'I know, it's a little scary to think about, having just decided that you aren't afraid to admit that you love me, even on dry land. And I think you're very sensible to be concerned.' He took her hands in his. 'Come and sit beside me and let me tell you a story,' he said, leading her over to sit on the edge of the bed.

'More make-believe?' Theresa asked, smiling at his serious expression.

'I wish it were,' Luke said. 'This is a true story.' He took a deep breath. 'Once upon a time, there were two young people who struck unbelievable sparks off of each other the first time that they met. Nothing like that had ever happened to either of them before, and in a few days they were sure it was love. In a few more days, they decided to marry. They were both brought up to believe that sex before marriage was wrong, and it was unthinkable that they live together beforehand, so naturally there was great inducement for them to marry quickly. Which they did. After the wedding, there wasn't much money, but the young husband was perfectly happy working on his writing at all hours, and making love to his young wife whenever they happened to be in bed at the same time. He didn't mind that she couldn't cook and didn't want children until they had more money. He didn't even notice that she grew more unhappy every day. He didn't realise that she hated never knowing when he'd want to eat. Or how much she hated that he forgot birthdays and anniversaries and left his clothes on the chairs and squeezed the toothpaste tube in the middle. She had no ambitions of her own, and didn't make friends easily. When the husband had some success and they started going to fancy parties, she was ill at ease. She accused him of flirting if he even spoke to a woman. She did find one thing, though, that made it all bearable. In fact, it turned her into a vivacious woman who couldn't resist using her newfound powers on any willing male.' He smiled sadly. 'I think you know what I mean.'

'Oh, Luke, I'm so sorry,' Theresa said, touched at the obvious sorrow the story of his unhappy marriage still caused him.

'So am I,' Luke said with a heavy sigh. 'The saddest thing of all is that, somewhere along the way, love died. I don't want that to happen to us. That's why I think it would be best if we took some time to be sure. I have no qualms about us living together, if you don't, but I want to save sex for that wonderful time when we might want to bring children into the world.' He looked at Theresa anxiously. 'You do want children, don't you?'

'Definitely,' Theresa replied. 'At least a couple. My mother's more than ready to be a grandmother.' She flung her arms around Luke and nestled her head against his shoulder. 'I'm so glad you told me all that. It helps me understand so many things about you. I wish you'd told me sooner.'

'God knows, I wanted to,' Luke said with feeling, 'but, realistically, there hasn't been a good time to do so before now. In California, I didn't want to involve you in my problems, and here...'

'I know,' Theresa interrupted, nodding. 'I didn't give you a chance before. But I don't think we'd have the kind of problems that you and Sonya did. I work strange hours sometimes, too, though, and might not be there to cook when you were hungry. Tell me, is it going to bother you to have a wife who's a detective? It already seems to worry you.'

'There, you see?' Luke said, gathering her close. 'Already a potential problem. Food's no problem. I can hire a cook. It's having you out alone that I don't like. I think I could handle it if you worked with a partner.'

'That,' Theresa said, kissing his chin, 'could be arranged. Which reminds me, partner, what are we going to do about Toby McDonald and his phony Louis Armstrong trumpet? Have you exhausted the supply of exotic dancers yet?'

'Not quite,' Luke replied. 'Shall we get to work?' He kissed Theresa's upturned nose. 'I'm afraid if we stay here much longer you'll undermine all of my good intentions.'

'Heaven forbid,' Theresa said teasingly. 'Let's check the last of the lovelies out, and then start on some of the smaller clubs. I have an idea that if Toby's settled in down here, he might frequent someplace more quiet than Bourbon Street.'

'Good idea,' Luke agreed. 'There's one other thing to check out first, though.'

'What's that?'

'You. Out of this hotel. No use wasting any more of A-1's money, is there?'

Theresa shook her head, and then giggled. 'Poor Quent. He's going to think I've lost my mind.'

'You have,' Luke said. 'And don't try to find it. I'm going to hide it, so that you'll never be able to escape me.'

* * *

Theresa moved back to Luke's apartment, this time winning the argument over where she would sleep.

'I don't think my upbringing provided me with the fortitude that yours gave you,' she told Luke, 'and I know a hold that would make you my helpless victim if I went berserk from frustration.'

Several days of searching for Toby McDonald proved fruitless, at last beginning to put a damper on the warm glow that Theresa felt at being continually blessed by the love that Luke now so freely showed her. Their only unexpected find had been the Brimstone brothers, behind the bar in a café near the river.

'We own part of this place,' William explained with a chuckle at Luke and Theresa's exclamations of surprise. 'Had a little luck in a poker game the night after we left you.'

'Don't know how long we'll stay here,' Wilber joined in, 'but so far we like it.'

When Theresa showed them Toby McDonald's picture, Wilber made a comment that she thought might prove helpful, but had so far produced nothing.

'Look how that guy's holding that trumpet,' he had remarked. 'He's holding it right. For playing it, I mean. I used to play a little myself, so I know.'

'Do you suppose,' Theresa had said later to Luke, 'that Toby might have tried to get work as a trumpet player? He didn't have all that much money, and once he got to New Orleans he apparently stopped using his credit cards.'

Luke shrugged. 'I don't know. It seems to me we'd have heard of any new trumpet players in the places where we've been.'

'I know.' Theresa chewed her lip thoughtfully. 'Try this scenario. You come down here, hoping to find your lady love, and she isn't here any more. All you've got is your wonderful trumpet and a love of jazz. You know you aren't good enough for the big time, so what do you do? My guess is you head for some tiny place way out in the sticks where you can make a few dollars and maybe get your meals free.'

'Sounds possible,' Luke replied. 'Or you get yourself a shack down by the bayou, a case of whisky, and wile away the hours playing for the alligators. Shall we start interviewing alligators to see if they've heard any bad trumpet-playing lately?'

'Oh, do be serious,' Theresa grumbled. 'Quent says I only have a couple more days to work on the case, and I hate to quit a loser. He couldn't get hold of Mrs McDonald to tell her what we did find out about Carmelita, and see if she wants us to continue. She's apparently gone on vacation.'

'That's funny,' Luke said. 'I thought . . .'

'What?'

Luke shrugged. 'Nothing. I just thought the woman would be glued to her telephone, waiting for you to call.'

'You would think she'd at least let us know where she was going, wouldn't you?' Theresa agreed.

Theresa was disconsolately poking at her breakfast on the last day on which she was officially on the McDonald case, when Luke suddenly thrust his newspaper in front of her.

'Look there,' he said, pointing to an advertisement. 'Maybe we should check that out tonight.'

' "Amateur night at Crawdaddy's",' Theresa read. ' "Prizes for the best solo and combo performances. Talent scouts guaranteed to be in the audience." ' She sighed. 'It's worth a try.'

'Come on, precious,' Luke said, giving her shoulders a squeeze. 'Look on the bright side. Even if we don't find McDonald there, we might get to hear the next Louis Armstrong give his première performance.'

'Or get to hear a lot of bad jazz,' Theresa said drily.

She tried to feel optimistic, but finally took a long walk to the French market so that she would not be hanging around the apartment looking gloomy while Luke was working on some writing he had recently started. When at last they arrived at Crawdaddy's, she was still depressed.

'I haven't seen you smile all day,' Luke complained. 'Are you sure it's that important that you find Toby McDonald? It's pretty obvious he doesn't want to be found.'

Theresa shook her head. 'No, I'm not sure. While I was walking today, I was thinking about that. I'm not sure I'm cut out for the detective business. I think all I want to do is get married so we can start having those children we were talking about.' She did smile at the radiant smile with which Luke greeted her statement. 'You like that idea?' she asked.

'Love it,' Luke said. 'But I don't think you should quit a loser. Besides, you may just be thinking that way because you're so down about this case. Come on, now, think positively. Say to yourself, Toby McDonald is sure to be here tonight. This is just the kind of place he'd be.'

'It is the kind of place I'd imagine he would be,' Theresa said, looking around. 'I wonder if they have a list of the contestants?'

'I'll see,' Luke replied. He returned shortly with a piece of paper in his hand. 'This is all they have,' he said, 'but the manager said that there are always more show up during the evening. Besides, he might be using a different name.'

'This could be a long night,' Theresa sighed. Toby McDonald's name was not on the list. Would she even recognise the man if he had changed his name?

When the contestants began playing, each gave his name and chatted briefly with the master of ceremonies about his background. Most were quite young, eager to launch their careers. They exhibited a wide range of talent. Some were very good, some dreadful. Theresa and Luke were soon caught up in the audience's loud and spontaneous response to the players. They were still applauding an especially good saxophone soloist, when a short, balding man got up from a table, walked up to the centre of the little stage and raised his trumpet. The master of ceremonies looked startled.

'Wait a minute, mister,' he said, moving towards the man as if to stop him. One long, sweet note, and both he and the audience fell silent. Theresa stared in disbelief, her heart pounding wildly.

'It's him,' she gasped, clutching at Luke's arm. 'Isn't it? Am I imagining things? And he's wonderful. Just wonderful.'

'That he is,' Luke agreed, staring intently at the man. He looked over at Theresa and smiled. 'I think you've found your man.'

When the man had finished playing the *St Louis Blues*, the audience would not let him go, in spite of the efforts of the master of ceremonies to get them to permit the next contestant to play. Finally, the man played a short, rousing version of *When The Saints Go Marching In*, bowed, and left the stage.

'Your name, sir,' called the master of ceremonies. 'You didn't give your name.'

'McDonald,' the man replied. 'Tobias McDonald.'

'It *is* him!' Theresa cried, smiling triumphantly at Luke.

'I never doubted it,' Luke replied, reaching over to squeeze her hand. 'Are you going to talk to him now?'

Theresa shook her head. 'Unless he starts to leave, I'll wait until the contest is over. He's sure to win a prize. I'd hate to spoil that for him. It may not make him very happy to hear that Josephine is on his trail.'

But, she was surprised to learn later, after Toby McDonald had indeed collected a prize and an offer of a regular job, he was not unhappy at all to hear that Josephine still loved him and wanted him back.

'If she wants to come down here and live with me, that's fine with me,' he said. 'I just decided it was time to do something I'd always wanted to do, before I got any older. I've wanted to play the trumpet since I was a wee little boy.' He smiled happily. 'I sure never thought I'd really make it. Do you think Josephine will want to come to New Orleans?'

'I certainly hope so,' Theresa said. She handed Toby the letter she had brought. 'Maybe this will give you a clue.'

Toby read the letter, his smile getting broader with each line he read. 'I'll be darned,' he said. 'I think she really loves me. I'll call her first thing in the morning.' The fact that his wife had been away did not concern him. 'She goes to visit her sister a lot,' he said. 'I'll call her there if she isn't at home.'

'How wonderful to have a happy ending,' Theresa said as she and Luke drove home. 'It was worth all of the trouble in the end, wasn't it?'

'Indeed it was,' Luke agreed. He smiled knowingly at Theresa. 'And now I'll bet you don't want to stop being a detective, after all.'

'Probably not,' Theresa admitted. 'I'll have to figure out how to work around raising a family. If I open my own agency in Hollywood and get some good people working for me, I should be able to do that. What do you think?'

Luke reached over and took Theresa's hand in his. 'I think you should do whatever will make you happy. Sometimes I disappear into my study for days at a time when I'm writing, and I don't think you would be happy unless you had a career of your own.'

Theresa squeezed Luke's hand and leaned her head against his shoulder. They were talking now as if they really were going to get married very soon. And, she thought, she was almost ready to tell Luke yes. Later, as she lay on her bed in her little Garden of Eden, basking in the afterglow of Luke's goodnight kiss, she decided that there was no reason to wait any longer to tell him that she thought they should get married. In the morning, she would tell him. She would send him off on an errand, make him a very special breakfast, and then tell him.

She was almost bursting with excitement the next morning, but she pretended to be unhappy about the fact that they had no fresh croissants for breakfast.

'Would you mind getting some?' she entreated, giving Luke her sweetest smile. 'I'm feeling very French this morning.'

'*Certainement, ma chérie,*' Luke replied. '*Veux-tu un melon aussi?*'

'Don't swamp me with your French,' Theresa giggled. 'If that means, do I want a melon, the answer is yes.'

'I will return *tout de suite*, my sweet,' Luke said, giving Theresa a quick kiss, '*avec des croissants et le melon.*'

When Luke had left, Theresa put on a lovely blue silk kimono that he had given her, then hurried to the kitchen, where she set the little table with a pretty lavender cloth, and Harry's finest china. She had just begun to whip the eggs for an omelette when the telephone rang.

'What a time for the phone to ring,' she grumbled, turning off the mixer. 'Hello!' she snapped crossly into the receiver. 'Oh, sorry, Quent. I was just in the middle of making an omelette,' she added when her brother commented on her grouchy tones.

'Well, I have some news that's apt to make you even grouchier,' he said. 'It's about the McDonald case.'

'Grouchy?' Theresa said. 'Why? I was going to call you in a little while and tell you the good news. I found Toby McDonald last night, playing the trumpet in an amateur contest. He's terrific.'

'Whoever he is, he may well be a terrific trumpet player,' Quent said drily. 'Brace yourself, Theresa. There are no Mr and Mrs Toby McDonald. Apparently they were both part of some more of Luke's games.'

Theresa stared at the receiver. Her hand started to shake. 'More... of Luke's games?' she repeated hoarsely.

'That's right. I found out... Theresa?' Quentin Long called his sister's name several times, but got no reply. The telephone had dropped from her shaking fingers.

'Oh, no!' Theresa cried, tears starting to stream down her cheeks. 'No!' she screamed. It couldn't be. Luke wouldn't have, he couldn't have done such a thing! But Quent wouldn't lie. It must be true. She hadn't found Toby McDonald at all. There was no happy ending to all of her work. It was nothing but another stupid, deceitful fraud that robbed her of all the pride she had taken in her success!

'I don't want to see him,' she cried aloud. 'I don't ever want to see that man again!' This time she was getting away from him and she would never come back. Never! She had to hurry. She ran into the bathroom, flung off her kimono, then pulled on jeans and a sweatshirt. Seeing her lipstick lying on the counter gave her an idea. She'd leave Luke a message he'd understand. She opened the lipstick and scrawled on the mirror, 'You louse! I hope you rot in hell!' Then she grabbed up her bag and ran out of the apartment, not caring which way she went as long as it was not where Luke Thorndike would be.

CHAPTER TEN

THERESA ran, tears still streaming down her cheeks, until she could run no more, and then jogged along, wiping her eyes from time to time on her sleeve. She dodged from one street to another, finally ending up in front of the Cabildo on Jackson Square. Luke would never think of looking for her in there, she thought, and went into the old building, joining a group who were taking a tour of the historic place which, the guide told them, had housed the likes of Jean LaFitte, the pirate, and the Marquis de La Fayette. Theresa scarcely heard, only dimly aware of her surroundings. All she could think, over and over, was, What shall I do? Dear God, what shall I do now?

She abandoned the group and slumped down on a bench on the second floor of the Cabildo. She buried her face in her hands, fighting down waves of nausea. The heat of her anger had faded. Nothing seemed to matter any more. Everything that had been beautiful and warm was now ugly and cold. She was alone again. Oh, God, she felt so alone! Would she ever feel happy again? Would she ever laugh? Would there ever be anyone like Luke to laugh with?

A heavy hand descending on Theresa's shoulder startled her so that she almost jumped out of her skin.

'Whoa, there!' said a raspy voice. 'Sorry, Theresa. I thought that was you. You OK?'

Theresa raised her head, staring at the familiar face of Orville Thompson peering into hers, his forehead serrated into a worried frown. 'Hello, Orville,' she said dully. 'No, I'm not OK.'

'Lovers' quarrel?' he asked, sitting down beside her.

'Not exactly,' Theresa replied. 'Worse than that.'

Orville clucked sympathetically. 'That's too bad. Mighty fine-looking young man, that Thorndike fellow. Want to tell me about it?'

Theresa shook her head. 'It's too complicated,' she said. 'It's all over, that's all.' Hearing herself speak those words brought forth a new flood of tears.

'Now, now, don't be so sure,' Orville said, patting her shoulder anxiously. 'Millie and me, we had some terrible fights when we were engaged, even when we were first married. Seems like it takes a while for two people to get adjusted, you know. Kind of like getting a new team of horses used to each other. You just take some time to think about things and then talk it over between you. It'll work out.'

'We've tried that before,' Theresa sobbed. 'It didn't help.'

'Someone tell you you only got so many tries?' Orville asked, peering into her face again.

'I don't want any more,' Theresa said stubbornly. 'I think I'd better just go home to Chicago.'

Orville shook his head. 'That won't fix anything,' he said. 'You'll no more'n get there and you'll change your mind.'

'No, I won't,' Theresa replied, frowning. She hiccuped loudly. 'Excuse me.'

'I'd wait until tomorrow, anyway,' Orville said. 'Don't rush off. Say, did you ever find that McDonald fellow?'

Those words sent a dagger of pain through Theresa's heart. 'There wasn't any McDonald fellow,' she said faintly. 'It was a hoax.'

'Well, how about that?' Orville said, shaking his head. 'You must run into some strange people in your business. Course, I do in mine, too. That's just life, I guess. Well, I've got to be going. Heading back to Dubuque today.' He stood up and looked out the windows. 'Back up the Mississippi. Same good old river at Dubuque as right out there.' He pointed across Jackson Square, then turned to Theresa. 'You know, Theresa,' he said, 'when Millie and I used to fight I'd go for a long walk along the river. It kind of helped me get things straight in my head. I'd look at all of that water, flowing on and on, forever and ever, and I'd feel kind of small. Pretty soon whatever we had our fight about didn't look so big, either. Maybe you ought to take a walk along the Mississippi, too.'

Theresa gave him a wavy smile. He was really a very nice man after all. 'Thanks, Orville. I might just try that. Have a good trip home.'

Orville nodded. 'It'll be OK. Kind of lonesome without Millie. She's only been gone a year, and I'm not used to it yet. Don't know quite how to act.' He gave Theresa an embarrassed smile. 'I guess you know about that,' he said. He reached into his pocket and pulled out a card. 'Let me know how things turn out for you, will you? I'd like to know.'

'I will,' Theresa promised, taking his card. She watched him go, then looked down at the card.

'Thompson's Garage and Café, Dubuque, Iowa,' she read, 'Orville and Millie Thompson, Proprietors.' Tears blurred her eyes once again. Orville had spent a lifetime with his Millie at his side, and she couldn't even get along with Luke for a few days. Was it really all Luke's fault, or was something wrong with her? She stood up and looked out the windows, then hurried down the stairs and across Jackson Square to the river.

Theresa climbed the ramp to the Moonwalk overlooking the Mississippi River and sat down on a bench. A freighter was passing, heading out to sea, and she watched it until it was out of sight past a bend in the river. Luke, she knew, would wonder where it was going, what it was carrying, and then make up some fanciful story about it. For the life of her, she couldn't think of anything clever at all. It was only an ordinary ship, carrying a prosaic load of grain or cotton to a regular destination. Without Luke, life was very dull and predictable. Maybe that was better. Theresa Long, she thought sadly, did not seem able to cope with anything that turned her predictions upside-down.

A young couple came on to the Moonwalk, so wrapped up in each other that they might as well have been in a closet. Theresa watched them nuzzling each other for a few minutes, and then got up and hurried back down the ramp, feeling close to tears again. She thrust her hands into her pockets and started walking along the street, hoping to find a place where she could watch the river without a reminder of blossoming love. At the foot of Canal Street she found such a place. An old-fashioned river-boat with a huge stern wheel was docked there, a sign inviting tourists to see New Orleans from the river. That, Theresa thought, was a perfect idea. If Luke was looking for her, he would never find her there, and she could watch the river to her heart's content, and see if it would bring her the same peace of mind it had brought to Orville Thompson.

She purchased a ticket and got on board, going to the top deck where she could stand at the rail and look out over the passing scene. As soon as the boat was under way, she knew she had made a good decision. Instead of watching the sights of New Orleans, she went to the stern and watched the paddle wheel churning the water, soothed by the wind in her hair and the slow, steady rhythm of the turning wheel.

By the time the boat returned to its dock, she had made another decision. While she loved Luke and always would, she could not marry him. It wouldn't be fair. Luke deserved someone better than she, someone who would not panic when he turned her life temporarily upside-down. Someone who could really learn to look at more than one side of a question before she reacted. It was obvious, when she thought about it, that the McDonald hoax was only another part of Luke's plan to win her back. He had meant no harm, had had no desire to hurt her. But she...she had never stopped to think until now. If it hadn't been for Orville Thompson, she might never have done so. Now, there was only one thing for her to do. She would return to Luke's apartment to get her things and to tell him goodbye. And to apologise for her hastily scrawled message.

She retraced her steps to Jackson Square, standing for a few minutes in the centre by the statue of Andrew Jackson, trying to get herself in the proper frame of mind for what she must do. All around the square were reminders of the past, and of people who had plunged ahead when their world turned upside-down and made historic victories of apparent disasters. Luke needed someone of that calibre by his side, not someone who saw only the easier negative every time.

'Thanks, Andrew,' Theresa said to the famous general, later President, astride his rearing horse. She started walking briskly, heading toward Luke's apartment.

She had not gone far when she felt a prickling sensation in the back of her neck. Someone was following her. She quickened her pace, trying to catch a glimpse of who it might be in the windows of the shops she passed. One was finally angled properly to mirror those behind her. She paused for a second. Coming along the pavement behind her were the Brimstone brothers.

How silly of me, she thought. They were no threat any more. She waited and then welcomed them with a smile.

'Hello, Wilber and William,' she said. 'How's your business going?'

Neither twin smiled. Instead, each took hold of one of Theresa's arms.

'Business is OK,' Wilber said, 'but we have something in mind to make us a little extra money. You come along with us and we'll explain what we mean.'

'Don't scream,' William said, poking something hard into Theresa's ribs.

'Is this some more of Luke's funny business?' Theresa demanded. 'Because if it is . . .'

'It isn't,' Wilber replied. 'This is our business.'

The twins hustled Theresa along until they came to a doorway, which opened on to stairs leading to the second floor of an old, ornate building with a wrought-iron balcony overlooking the street. At the top they paused, while Wilber opened the door to an apartment. They propelled Theresa across the room and deposited her on a chair. William quickly tied her hands and feet, while she glowered at them silently.

'Now, then,' Wilber said, drawing up a chair in front of her, 'you listen to me, and stop frowning like that. No one's going to hurt you, and you're going to come out of this a lot better than you are right now.'

'Meaning what?' Theresa asked coldly.

'Meaning you're going to end up back with Luke, like you oughta be, instead of running around like a squawking hen who's had her tail feathers stepped on.'

'I thought you said Luke didn't put you up to this,' Theresa said. 'It's pretty obvious that he did.'

William shook his head. 'No, ma'am. Luke came into our bar this afternoon and told us a lot of things while he was drinking a little too much. See, when he saw the telephone off the hook and saw your message, he kind of figured what had happened, so he called your brother and found out he was right. I don't think I ever saw a man so shook up.'

Tears came to Theresa's eyes and trickled down her cheeks. 'I was going back to tell him I'm sorry,' she said.

'I don't think that's what he wants to hear,' said Wilber.

'What do you mean?'

'He's pretty well convinced that you don't really love him,' Wilber replied.

'But I do!' Theresa cried. 'It's just that . . . I'm not good enough for him.'

Wilber and William looked at each other. 'That might be,' William said, 'but you're the one he wants. At least, it sure seemed that way at first. Then, after a while, he started talking like he wasn't so sure. But we decided he probably didn't mean that part, it was just the bourbon talking, so that's when we took him home and made up our plan.'

'What plan?' Theresa demanded.

The twins smiled at each other.

'Just listen. You'll see,' Wilber replied as William went to the telephone.

'Hello, Thorndike?' William said a few moments later. 'How you feeling? That's good. Say, I've got a little proposition for you. We've got Theresa here. If you can come up with ten grand in a couple of hours, you can have her back. Otherwise, we might make her disappear kind of permanently.'

'He won't believe that,' Theresa said while William listened to Luke's reply. 'You two aren't killers.'

'Don't be too sure,' Wilber said smugly, with a leer that gave Theresa a sick feeling in the pit of her stomach. 'We've done some pretty shady stuff in the past.'

'OK,' William said at last. 'We'll bring her right over.' He hung up the phone and grinned at his brother. 'He's gonna write us a cheque. I think I trust him, don't you?'

'Sure,' Wilber agreed.

'This,' Theresa said, as Wilber untied her, 'is the phoniest set-up I ever saw. Extortionists don't take cheques. Why don't you just admit that Luke told you he'd pay you to help find me and then put me through this charade? I'm getting used to it now. It doesn't bother me in the slightest.'

William shook his head. 'The condition he was in when we took him home, he couldn't think up anything like this. I was afraid he wouldn't be able to figure out what I was talking about, but he sounds a little better now. Come on, let's get going.'

During the short walk to Luke's apartment, the twins kept a firm grip on Theresa, even though she insisted she would not run away. They were, she decided, determined to keep pretending, in spite of the fact that she knew what they were doing. Poor Luke. He must have had a miserable day. Even worse than hers. And it was all her fault. Now, if she told him she was leaving... She blinked back fresh tears. Somehow when she made her decision she hadn't pictured him drowning his sorrows in the Brimstones' bar, if that was really true.

When Luke answered Wilber's brisk knock, she could see that it was. He looked haggard, his eyes red and puffy. He eyed Theresa warily, as the twins, still holding her firmly, escorted her into his living-room.

'Signed, sealed, and delivered as promised,' William said.

Luke nodded and held out a cheque. 'Turn her loose,' he said quietly, as William took the cheque from him and then handed it to Wilber, 'and then get out of here. I don't think much of people who turn on a friend when he's down.'

'One more thing, first,' Wilber said, thrusting Theresa toward Luke. 'We want to see you kiss her.'

Theresa stared at Luke, who looked startled by the request. Luke looked at her for a moment and then back at Wilber. 'I'm not sure she wants me to,' he said, his expression drawn and unhappy.

His obvious misery was too much for Theresa. 'Yes, I do!' she cried, throwing her arms around him and looking up into his dear face, her eyes misty. 'If you want to,' she added in a faint voice, as he looked at her doubtfully. 'I know I don't deserve it.'

Very slowly, Luke's arms encircled Theresa, almost as if he thought she were too fragile to touch. Then, as his head bent toward her and she smiled, they crushed her to him. His mouth found hers, tentative at first, and then with increasing pressure as he felt Theresa respond.

At the first moment that Luke's lips touched hers, Theresa knew that she could never tell him goodbye. She might not deserve him, but she could try, and she had learned one very important lesson that day. Having Luke happy was more important to her than anything else in the world. If he still loved her and wanted to marry her, she was his.

For a long time, Luke and Theresa clung to each other, oblivious to the presence of the Brimstone brothers. At last Luke raised his head and smiled crookedly at Theresa. 'Do you think that will satisfy them?' he asked.

Theresa looked back at the twins, who were smiling happily.

'That's more like it,' William said. 'When are you two going to get married? We'd like to be there.'

'As soon as the law allows,' Theresa replied, 'if Luke still wants me.' She held her breath, waiting for Luke's reply.

He smiled slowly. 'Do I ever,' he replied, giving her a bone-crushing hug. Then he frowned at the Brimstones. 'I don't know if we ought to invite you or not. I'm grateful to you for bringing her back, but . . .' he smiled at Theresa again, 'I think she might have come back on her own.'

Wilber chuckled and handed the cheque back to William, who calmly tore it up and gave the pieces to Luke.

'We just wanted to see this all turned out right,' William said. 'See, it's this way,' he added, grinning at Theresa's puzzled look. 'When we met Luke back in Hollywood, he told us how much he loved you, and then he told us about the story he made up about how he might get you to marry him. He only had one guy who was supposed to be after him in that story, but we talked him into letting us do it because we kind of liked the idea of being in on something like that.' He chuckled. 'I guess we're a lot more romantic about things than we look, because when Luke told us he thought it had all fallen apart we couldn't stand it. We wanted him to have the happy ending like he'd planned. Maybe you'd have come back, but we wanted to be sure.'

Theresa looked up at Luke, whose eyes were now sparkling with their old devilish fires as he grinned at

William. 'I never saw two more unlikely cupids,' he said, 'but we'll be honoured if you'll come to our wedding. We'll let you know as soon as things are set.'

After the twins had left, Luke returned to Theresa's side, his expression now so sober that she feared he had only pretended to want to marry her to please the Brimstones. She was even more worried when he took a tight hold of her hand and frowned at her.

'Young lady,' he said, turning and pulling her swiftly along behind him through the bedroom, and into the mirrored bath, 'we have some serious talking to do. I've been to hell and back today.' He pointed at Theresa's message on the mirrors. 'That,' he said sternly, 'is inexcusable. From now on, yell at me if you want to and call me names, but don't write things on the walls and then run away so that I can't defend myself.'

'Yes, sir,' Theresa replied meekly, relieved that there was still going to be a 'from now on'. 'What I did was awful and stupid. You must think I'll never get any sense. Let me get something to clean that off with.'

'Just leave it for now,' Luke said, shaking his head. 'Maybe it will help remind you not to do it again.'

'Oh, I won't,' Theresa said earnestly. 'I promise. I'll stop and think why you did something, instead. I'm still not exactly sure why you did that trick with the McDonalds, but...' she smiled tentatively at Luke's still stern expression, 'I'm sure it has something to do with that story William was talking about.'

'Only partly,' Luke replied. He studied Theresa's face, his own softening, his slow, beautiful smile gradually spreading its light into the dark depths of his eyes. 'Let's get comfortable. I plan to do a lot of talking, and then . . .' he swept Theresa into his arms and placed a quick kiss on her lips, 'I plan to invent a new maxim: if the third time fails, the fourth time will definitely be the charmed one.' With that, he carried Theresa into the bedroom, and set her carefully down on the huge, round bed. While she watched, her pulse quickening at the knowledge that this remarkable man was going to be truly hers in spite of everything, he flung off his shirt and then stretched out beside her and took her into his arms again. 'Comfortable?' he asked.

'Comfortable?' Theresa repeated dreamily. 'Oh, Luke, if only you knew how terrible I've felt all day and how wonderful I feel now.' She caressed his dark hair back from his forehead gently. 'That was a silly thing to say. You do know, don't you?' she answered her own question.

Luke nodded. 'I was afraid we might never be here again.' He kissed Theresa's cheek, then rubbed his own cheek against hers. 'I don't know if I could have stood that,' he said huskily. 'I love you so very much. The only reason I invented a Toby McDonald was to make you happy. I knew how much it meant to you to find him, and you were getting so discouraged.'

'You mean,' Theresa said, 'that there wasn't supposed to be any Toby McDonald in your story? I don't understand. Why don't you start at the beginning and tell me everything?' She lifted her head so that she could see Luke's face, and the love she saw there made her forget her question and press her lips to his in a kiss that she could scarcely bear to end.

At last Luke framed her face with his hands and whispered, his mouth still touching hers. 'There's someone watching us.'

'There is?' Theresa drew back, startled, and looked around, then made a face as Luke chuckled and pointed toward the mirror overhead. 'Oh, them,' she said. 'They don't count.'

'Sure they do,' Luke replied. 'That's Thorny Lukewarm and Dr Theresa Longfreud again. They're really the sex inspectors from the planet Libido, here to see if the fourth time really is the charm. If we don't get this talking nonsense over with, they're apt to become very upset and unleash some of those evil weapons that Libido is famous for.'

'Heaven forbid,' Theresa said, giggling. The sound of her own laughter made her suddenly realise how long it seemed since she had last felt like laughing. Without Luke, she wondered if she ever would have. 'Oh, Luke,' she said, burying her face against his neck, 'I love you so much. It didn't take me long today to realise how wrong I'd been. But I almost made a terrible mistake. I might not have come back to stay. I thought you deserved someone better. I still think maybe you do, but if you can stand me, I think I've learned a little more again. Maybe some day soon I won't panic if I find out something I thought was real was only a game.'

'And maybe,' Luke said wryly, 'I'll learn which kind of games not to play. Although I was sort of stuck with Toby after I'd started you searching for him in the first place. You see, the first thing my story required was to get you to New Orleans, since I was planning to be here, so I invented Josephine

McDonald and her missing husband, and hired an actress I used to know in California, but who now lives in Chicago, to take the part of Josephine. I didn't plan on having you find Toby. I wanted to sweep you off your feet again and have you forget all about him after a while. When I saw that wasn't going to work out, I adjusted the story accordingly. That was the way the whole story worked, you see. The outline was there, but we had several options, depending on what actually happened. For instance, I didn't know whether you'd fly or take the train.'

'I wondered about that,' Theresa exclaimed. 'I thought you must have had a detective watching me to find out. All you really needed was to talk to Josephine, wasn't it?'

'That's right. And to do a little sleight of hand with some tickets to get one that looked as if it was for the same room as you had. I didn't know if the opportunity would present itself for the Brimstones to get their message across on the train, either. If they didn't, they'd have done it in some bar or restaurant after you got here. We weren't sure exactly how long to string out their threat, or what form their attack would take. We had a few surprises, too.' Luke paused and chuckled. 'I knew you'd probably learned some self-defence in order to become a private investigator, but I didn't realise what a dynamo you are. Wilber complained afterwards that, if he'd known, he wasn't sure he'd have taken the job. And, of course, there was that crazy grapefruit. I didn't know whether the twins had decided to ad lib something new or there really was someone after me.' He hugged Theresa tightly.

'That night turned out better than it would have without the grapefruit, didn't it?'

'Mmm,' Theresa replied, sighing as Luke insinuated his hand beneath her sweatshirt. 'Wait a minute,' she said. She sat up and pulled the sweatshirt off. 'There, that's better. I like the way you feel, my love.' She pressed against Luke suggestively.

Luke cleared his throat and placed his hand on Theresa's breast. 'Now, as I was saying...what was I saying?'

Theresa giggled again, her heart now so light that she felt she might float into space with Luke beside her. 'Something about what you'd planned and what you didn't plan,' she replied. 'I hope you didn't plan on my winding up in gaol for car theft, or was Patsy Muffett leaving her keys here and her car out in front part of your plan?'

Luke slid a mischievous glance from beneath his long lashes. 'Maybe I'll just let you wonder about that. Ouch!' as Theresa pinched him. 'Don't hit me,' he said, pretending fear. 'I confess. That was a stroke of luck.'

'Luck?' Theresa scowled, and then burst out laughing at the devilment in Luke's eyes. 'Luke Thorndike, you are terrible,' she said. 'Go on, finish your blasted story. Dr Longfreud is getting restless.'

'And Thorny is anything but lukewarm,' Luke replied, pulling Theresa closer to him and demonstrating with a suggestive movement of his hips against hers. 'There's not much more to tell. The plan was to have you find out about the threat. If you hadn't found out on the train and moved right in, you'd have known where to find me and come rushing to my side.

I'd woo you while the Brimstones stalked me. Eventually they'd make their move, which would be serious enough to scare you into realising that you loved me but would somehow be bungled so that you wouldn't call the police. I didn't count on you falling under my spell quite so fast.' He grinned and kissed the tip of Theresa's nose. 'And I definitely didn't think you'd be angry to find out I wasn't really in danger. I guess I'm condemned to join that legion of men who admit that they'll never really understand a woman's mind.'

'Hmph,' Theresa said, toying with the dark curls of hair on Luke's chest. 'I don't think you're any easier to understand. How on earth did you ever come up with the idea of writing a story for us to play out?'

'A rather famous fellow gave me the thought,' Luke replied. 'Will Shakespeare. Remember the lines from *As You Like It*? "All the world's a stage. And all the men and women merely players: They have their exits and their entrances; And one man in his time plays many parts." Ignoring the profound wisdom that follows, I thought to myself one day that I didn't like the part I was assigned or the part you were playing, so far away from me. I'd heard about Carl Weidenkamp. At first, I thought that if you'd found the right man I shouldn't interfere. Then I decided to check him out, and see if I thought he was the right man for you.' Luke paused and grinned devilishly. 'Once I'd met him, there was no way I could let you waste your life on that dullard. I decided to do some rewriting of both our scripts.'

'That was rather presumptuous of you,' Theresa said teasingly. 'I don't think I appreciate your lack of confidence in my judgement.'

Luke chuckled. 'I was pretty confident that once we were together again you'd see the light. Naturally, I was delighted that you saw it without my help. That led me to hope that maybe you'd learned enough about men in five years to be over being angry with me. If you'd welcomed me with open arms, I'd never have used the Brimstone brothers at all. Of course, that would have spoiled my story. Do you think you'd have liked it better that way?'

'I don't know,' Theresa said thoughtfully. 'I can't even imagine it happening that way. A happy ending with no story. Would you have liked it better?'

'I don't think so,' Luke replied. 'We've had some bad moments, but I think we've both learned a lot about each other. That can't help but be a good thing.'

'I think you're right about that,' Theresa said, leaning across Luke and smiling down at him. 'And now you have your happy ending and your story is finished.'

'Oh, no, never finished,' Luke replied. 'Only the first act, for us. And I do have some more work to do on the first act, too.'

'Now what?' Theresa asked, pretending to look severe. 'Am I going to go through a wedding, only to discover that the minister is really not a minister, after all?'

'Never that,' Luke said seriously. 'We will have the most official wedding that ever was. No, my love, I'm going to turn our story, just as it happened, into a screenplay. Of course, the names will be changed to protect us innocents, and most of the parts will be played by actors, but I think the Brimstones will be terrific as themselves, don't you?'

'Fantastic,' Theresa agreed. She lay across Luke, her breasts responding with a tantalising feeling of swollen longing to the roughness of his chest beneath her. 'Darling love,' she said huskily, 'are you through talking yet? I think Dr Longfreud just zapped me with something from Libido.' She let her hand stray below Luke's waist. 'I think she got you, too.'

'Mmm,' Luke sighed. 'Do that again. Oh, yes . . .' He smiled dreamily at Theresa. 'Why don't you take off the rest of my clothes for me, caressing as you go? I've always dreamed of having you do that. Then I'll do the same for you.'

'All right,' Theresa said softly. She got to her knees and carefully unzipped Luke's trousers, slowly pulling them down, taking time to answer his request with gentle hands. By the time she had finished, she was so aroused that she felt that her entire body was trembling with desire. When Luke knelt astride her and kissed each new spot he uncovered as he removed her jeans, she felt as if sky-rockets were exploding both inside and out, dazzling her with sensations so overwhelming that she could scarcely breath. She held out her arms, and Luke lowered himself into them, devouring her with a kiss of such passionate hunger that Theresa gave a deep moan of longing. 'Oh, Luke,' she murmured, 'I love you so. I can't live without you any longer. Please . . .'

'Yes,' Luke said hoarsely. 'Now the time is right.' He entered her carefully, gently, as she knew he would. Then, as she arched toward him eagerly, he let the full fire of his passion have its way, sweeping the world away until they had reached that special world where lovers find release.

Afterwards, Luke lay beside her, his hands stroking her with delicate tenderness, his mouth feathering her with light kisses. 'It's something to go from hell to heaven in one day, isn't it?' he murmured.

'Mmm-hmm,' Theresa agreed, her hands exploring Luke's lean, hard body with a new possessiveness. 'All in all, I think I'd rather stay in heaven.'

Luke smiled. 'I think we can stay there for a while,' he said, tucking Theresa close and angling one leg across her, 'but even that might get boring eventually. I heard of a fellow who tried it. He found this strange, golden gate right in the middle of an empty car park, and when he opened it . . .'

Theresa sighed contentedly and wiggled her hips against Luke, feeling him begin to respond again. No place on heaven or earth would be boring with Luke Thorndike for company. It was like having a magical gate, behind which lurked continual, fantastic surprises. Only a fool would be afraid to enter that gate, and she was no longer afraid.

'Theresa,' Luke said softly, 'are you listening?'

'I was trying,' she replied, 'but it was hard. All I could think of was how much I love you and how happy I'm going to be married to you. Would you mind starting over?'

'Never mind,' Luke said, his eyes filled with love. 'I like your story better. Say that again.'

Theresa did.

HARLEQUIN
Romance

Coming Next Month

#3019 THE SNOW GARDEN Bethany Campbell
Hedy Hansen needs to ignore Christmas and the painful memories the season
brings. But she hasn't reckoned with her new Holly Street neighbors,
especially the irrepressible Ty Marek.

#3020 FOLLY TO LOVE Lynn Jacobs
Ross Courtenay always comes along at the right time—and Olivia has never
needed his helping hand more than now. But can she just close her eyes and
let him take over her life—especially after he's admitted his
dishonorable intentions?

#3021 LETTERS OF LOVE Judy Kaye
Too many letters are complicating Kate Matthew's life. There's her
correspondence with the mysterious C.G. of Chicago, and her letters about
nurses' rights to Dr. Chase Kincaid, her boss at St. Mike's Hospital in Fargo.
And then, there are the love letters written by Chase—to his ex-wife.

#3022 RIDDELL OF RIVERMOON Miriam MacGregor
Ten years after her mother and aunt had parted in anger, Fleur, at Luke
Riddell's request, comes to Rivermoon to help her Aunt Jessica. Only hoping to
end the family feud, Fleur can't understand why Luke should mistrust
her motives.

#3023 LET ME COUNT THE WAYS Leigh Michaels
Sara Prentiss has found a haven in New England's Chandler College and in
Olivia Reynolds, the mother she's longed for. Then famous thriller writer
Adam Merrill arrives—and finds a mystery right in the middle of Sara's
peaceful little world!

#3024 THE FATEFUL BARGAIN Betty Neels
Sebastian van Tecqx provides the solution to Emily's most pressing problem—
in return for her temporary help with his convalescent sister in Delft. Emily
knows it's hopeless, but with Sebastian's constant presence, she can't stop
herself falling in love.

Available in December wherever paperback books are sold, or
through Harlequin Reader Service:

In the U.S.
901 Fuhrmann Blvd.
P.O. Box 1397
Buffalo, N.Y. 14240-1397

In Canada
P.O. Box 603
Fort Erie, Ontario
L2A 5X3

CHRISTMAS IS FOR KIDS

Spend this holiday season with nine very special children. Children whose wishes come true at the magical time of Christmas.

Read American Romance's CHRISTMAS IS FOR KIDS— heartwarming holiday stories in which children bring together four couples who fall in love. Meet:

Frank, Dorcas, Kathy, Candy and Nicky—They become friends at St. Christopher's orphanage, but they really want to be adopted and become part of a real family, in #321 *A Carol Christmas* by Muriel Jensen.

Patty—She's a ten-year-old certified genius, but she wants what every little girl wishes for: a daddy of her own, in #322 *Mrs. Scrooge* by Barbara Bretton.

Amy and Flash—Their mom is about to deliver their newest sibling any day, but Christmas just isn't the same now—not without their dad. More than anything they want their family reunited for Christmas, in #323 *Dear Santa* by Margaret St. George.

Spencer—Living with his dad and grandpa in an all-male household has its advantages, but Spence wants Santa to bring him a mommy to love, in #324 *The Best Gift of All* by Andrea Davidson.

These children will win your hearts as they entice—and matchmake—the adults into a true romance. This holiday, invite them—and the four couples they bring together—into your home.

Look for all four CHRISTMAS IS FOR KIDS books coming in December from Harlequin American Romance. And happy holidays!

XMAS-KIDS-1

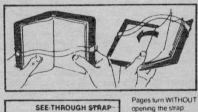

HARLEQUIN'S "BIG WIN"
SWEEPSTAKES RULES & REGULATIONS
NO PURCHASE NECESSARY TO ENTER OR RECEIVE A PRIZE

1. To enter and join the Harlequin Reader Service, scratch off the pink metallic strips on all your BIG WIN tickets #1-#6. This will reveal the values for each sweepstakes entry number, the number of free books you will receive and your free bonus gift as part of our Reader Service. If you do not wish to take advantage of our introduction to the Harlequin Reader Service but wish to enter the Sweepstakes only, scratch off the pink metallic strips on your BIG WIN tickets #1-#4 only. To enter, return your entire sheet of tickets intact. Incomplete and/or inaccurate entries are not eligible for that section or section(s) of prizes. Not responsible for mutilated or unreadable entries or inadvertent printing errors. Mechanically reproduced entries are null and void.

2. Either way your unique Sweepstakes numbers will be compared against the list of winning numbers generated at random by the computer. In the event that all prizes are not claimed, random drawings will be held from all entries received from all presentations to award all unclaimed prizes. All cash prizes are payable in U.S. funds. This is in addition to any free, surprise or mystery gifts that might be offered. The following prizes are awarded in this sweepstakes: *Grand Prize (1) $1,000,000; First Prize (1) $35,000; Second Prize (1) $10,000; Third Prize (3) $5,000; Fourth Prize (10) $1,000; Fifth Prize (25) $500; Sixth Prize (5000)$5.

   *This Sweepstakes contains a Grand Prize offering of a $1,000,000 annuity. Winner may elect to receive $25,000 a year for 40 years without interest totalling $1,000,000 or $350,000 in one cash payment. Entrants may cancel Reader Service at any time without cost or obligation to buy (see details in center insert card).

3. Extra Bonus Prize: This presentation offers two extra bonus prizes valued at $30,000 each to be awarded in a random drawing from all entries received.

4. Versions of this Sweepstakes with different graphics will be offered in other mailings or at retail outlets by Torstar Corp. and its affiliates. This promotion is being conducted under the supervision of Marden-Kane, Inc., an independent judging organization. By entering this Sweepstakes, each entrant accepts and agrees to be bound by these rules and the decisions of the judges, which shall be final and binding. Odds of winning in the random drawing are dependent upon the total number of entries received. Taxes, if any, are the sole responsibility of the winners. Prizes are non-transferable. All entries must be received by March 31, 1990. The drawing will take place on or about April 30, 1990 at the offices of Marden-Kane, Inc., Lake Success, NY.

5. This offer is open to residents of the U.S., the United Kingdom and Canada, 18 years or older except employees of Torstar Corp., its affiliates, subsidiaries, Marden-Kane, Inc. and all other agencies and persons connected with conducting this Sweepstakes. All Federal, State and local laws apply. Void wherever prohibited or restricted by law.

6. Winners will be notified by mail and may be required to execute an affidavit of eligibility and release that must be returned within 14 days after notification. Canadian winners will be required to answer a skill-testing question. Winners consent to the use of their name, photograph and/or likeness for advertising and publicity in conjunction with this and similar promotions without additional compensation.

7. For a list of our most current major prize winners, send a stamped, self-addressed envelope to: WINNERS LIST c/o MARDEN-KANE, INC., P.O. BOX 701, SAYREVILLE, NJ 08871.

If Sweepstakes entry form is missing, please print your name and address on a 3″ × 5″ piece of plain paper and send to:

In the U.S.

Harlequin's "BIG WIN" Sweepstakes
901 Fuhrmann Blvd.
Box 1867
Buffalo, NY 14269-1867

In Canada

Harlequin's "BIG WIN" Sweepstakes
P.O. Box 609
Fort Erie, Ontario
L2A 5X3

LTY-H119

Wonderful, luxurious gifts can be yours with proofs-of-purchase from any specially marked "Indulge A Little" Harlequin or Silhouette book with the Offer Certificate properly completed, plus a check or money order (do not send cash) to cover postage and handling payable to Harlequin/Silhouette "Indulge A Little, Give A Lot" Offer. We will send you the specified gift.

Mail-in-Offer

OFFER CERTIFICATE

Item:	A. Collector's Doll	B. Soaps in a Basket	C. Potpourri Sachet	D. Scented Hangers
# of Proofs-of -Purchase	18	12	6	4
Postage & Handling	$3.25	$2.75	$2.25	$2.00
Check One				

Name _____

Address _____ Apt. # _____

City _____ State _____ Zip _____

ONE PROOF OF PURCHASE

To collect your free gift by mail you must include the necessary number of proofs-of-purchase plus postage and handling with offer certificate.

HR-2

Harlequin®/Silhouette®

Mail this certificate, designated number of proofs-of-purchase and check or money order for postage and handling to:

INDULGE A LITTLE
P.O. Box 9055
Buffalo, N.Y. 14269-9055